SENTENCED TO LIFE

by Sherry Boswell

DORRANCE
PUBLISHING CO
EST. 1920
PITTSBURGH, PENNSYLVANIA 15238

Dorrance Publishing Co
585 Alpha Drive
Suite 103
Pittsburgh, PA 15238
Visit our website at *www.dorrancebookstore.com*

ISBN: 978-88-85272-13-2
eISBN: 978-8-8852-7669-6

SENTENCED TO LIFE

ABOUT THE AUTHOR

Born and raised in Memphis, TN, the sixth of seven children, I'm a twin as well. Upon graduating from high school a year late, I was already a mother, too young to even care for myself, didn't have a clue about life, not to mention that I had never heard of the facts of life (birds and the bees). Probably thought that was a book, having said that, when I became pregnant a lightbulb went off in my head. I made a choice to be the best mother I could be. I already had a deep love for babies and I had some experience beginning at the age of eight years old, and I had lots of hands-on experience at the age of 13. On my own, I began to realize this big responsibility that was all mine. You know how the story goes with the guys, it didn't matter to me because I was wise beyond my years and could do it on my own. So what can I say about my first pregnancy (young) and my second at the age of 25 (dumb)?

So I would like to say to teenagers, make better choices, choose abstinence. Abstain until you are married, if at all possible, in the event you fall off course be wise about it, you don't need to continue to have babies alone (single), don't think that sleeping with a guy means he loves you, it's just what it says. When it comes to him playing a role in being a parent, it's probably not going to happen. Be very selective in choosing a partner, meaning find out about his upbringing, where he's from, and most importantly if he has a relationship with God. If he is the guy for you he will understand your stance and he should have the same morals and values.

Have a plan for your life, for starting a family. Don't expect parents to become

parents again. Think and pray about the life you choose to live. Ask yourself, can I afford to take this leap? Remember, once it's done you can't reverse it. Pray and ask God for directions. Think you are not making a choice of which movie to see, you're making at the very least an eighteen-year decision.

THINK, THINK.

*Sherry - **Sentenced to Life***

CHAPTER 1

It was a nice, cool spring afternoon in the home of the Tirans in an affluent area of Atlanta. Not long before the graduation of the only son of Judge Walter and chief heart surgeon Dr. Elizabeth Tirans, he was also following in their footsteps by being the valedictorian of his class. Everyone was excited and preparing for his walk down the aisle and to see him receive the many awards that he worked for. He didn't want them to hear the speech; he wanted it to be a surprise so he kept it in the car because everyone's attention was on him. Rosalita, the chef, had the table set for dinner and was calling them all in to be seated. It was very rare that they all got to sit down to dinner together; they had to take advantage of this. There was one problem: They sat waiting on Anna Beth, their 15-year-old daughter, who was a sophomore in high school. No one seemed to know where she was, and did she have cheerleading practice that she forgot to tell us about? We asked Symie, the nanny, if she had said anything to her before she left this morning, saying no, we decided to call her cell phone, but no answer. We finally decided to have dinner without her thinking she would soon show up. Little did they know she had been sneaking around with this young guy that lived in the projects on the other side of town.

With their parents having such a busy schedule, they rarely had time for each other, and hardly ever for their children, they had their own phone, cars, credit cards, and every other gadget imaginable. This was the way they tried to make up for their absence.

Elizabeth wasn't able to have mother/daughter talks with Beth, Symie was the only one she had to talk to or share life's issues with, as far as they knew she was still a virgin. After they were done with dinner they moved to the family room to call Beth's phone again. They were very concerned, it was 7:45 at night, according to Symie she was never out this late without someone knowing. Just as they picked up the phone to call again she walked in the door.

Elizabeth jumped to her feet and asked, "Where have you been? We had all begun to worry about you."

Beth was surprised to see everyone at home because that didn't happen often, she had to think fast. "I was out with some friends. We decided to get something to eat after practice."

"So you forgot to tell Symie this morning? As luck would have it I wasn't scheduled for rounds this afternoon and once things were going okay, so I was glad some of my assistants could handle the load, I called home to have dinner set up for us and when you didn't show up I was disappointed, it's not often that we can have a family dinner. Hopefully it won't be as long as it has been, okay?"

"Okay, Mom, I'm sorry I wasn't here, we have been practicing for the competition in two months."

Just then Beth's cell phone rang and she excused herself to take the call.

"Why would she leave the room in such a rush?" she asked her husband. "She always takes her calls from her friends in front of us. She looked awfully strange when she looked at the caller ID, then immediately rushed off."

Little did anybody know that Beth had not been at practice for a while, she was almost about to get kicked off the squad for failing to show up. She had been with Peshun because she needed to tell him she had missed her cycle for two months. She was scared, didn't know what to do. He was trying to convince her to tell her mother, but she was afraid to.

They didn't have a connection; her mother was busy, and they had never had a mother-daughter discussion. So he was calling to see what she was going to do. He told his grandmother because she had always been there for him. She suggested that she sit down with her parents and let them know what was going on. It would not be a secret for long, if she was actually pregnant. Being that they were this very prominent family that everyone knew and if they didn't know them they had heard of them. They thought that providing the lifestyle they had and all the things they gave them made up for their absence. Not having time with the kids showed that they didn't know what was going on in their lives, much less who they were hanging out with. The one thing she always said to Beth was to "Never date or talk to any boys from the projects." She always suggested for her to talk with some of the ladies' sons in the exclusive bridge and society clubs.

Lately on her way out the door, going to the hospital, she glanced at the kids. Jr. was on cloud nine, thinking about his graduation, and Beth seemed a little bit reserved. She was planning on having a talk with her, but it seemed like she never had the time. She and her husband agreed; the boys will talk, and the girls will talk. Not realizing that they both should have a relationship with them. So Peshun asked her again what was she going to do; he had let her know over and over that he was in this with her and that he wouldn't leave her to deal with this alone. She was also afraid that she did what her mother asked her not to do. Not only did she give in and have a relationship with the boy from the projects, she had been sleeping with him for about ten months now. She knew her mother was going to disown her. She had never understood why her own mother disliked people that lived in the projects. My feelings were just because they didn't have what we had, and they were still human. Peshun had always made me feel special and treated me with the utmost respect. He worked at McDonald's and I didn't have to work at all.

When I asked my parents about a job after school, they said I was ungrateful. They felt as if they were giving us more than we could ask for. I felt that I wanted a job because neither one of them were ever home, and I always felt alone. I could always talk to the staff; in fact, all of them made me feel welcome to come to them if I needed to. I did when I was younger, but sometimes you need your own mother to make you feel special and loved. So then, I told Peshun that now was a bad time because Jr. was graduating in three days and everyone was focused on him and the big dinner that was planned at one of the top hotels. If I had to tell what was going on, it would be after all the graduation stuff.

Just then, Jr. rushed into my room to discuss all the activities and then I said, "KeKe, I will call you back." I didn't confide in my brother, because I felt he would tell. I could trust him, but I just couldn't tell him. He was so excited about everything, and I didn't want to interfere with his happiness. Well, a few days later everyone was getting dressed for the festivities, when the phone rang and it was the cheerleading coach. She had been telling Beth to have one of her parents call her. As luck would have it, Beth was by the phone and answered it quickly.

"Hello?"

"Beth, this is Coach Blaine, I haven't heard from your parents, have you been giving them my messages?"

"Yes, but you know how busy they are, they're getting ready for my brother's graduation in three hours, and I promise."

"Oh, I'm sorry," said Coach Blaine. "I wasn't thinking about tonight being graduation, so I apologize for calling, but I really don't know what has gotten into you, you were so excited at first and would always be ready for a good practice, now you never show up. I've given you ample chances but to no avail, are you sure everything is okay?"

"I'm positive, just kind of dealing with teenage issues at the present. I give you my word, I will be back on track next week."

"I hope so, because I will be calling back to speak to one of your parents."

"I won't disappoint you, Coach Blaine."

"I hope not."

"I have to run and start getting dressed, goodbye."

I hung up the phone and erased the number from the caller ID. I went to my room and sat on my bed for a minute to collect my thoughts before getting ready. I said, "What have I done?" How could I have been so careless? Whatever made me think that this couldn't happen to me? If I just had to sleep with Peshun we should have used protection. I could afford it even if he couldn't. I would never, ever want to be caught purchasing them. Shun was trying to convince me to have a meeting with my parents, and his grandmother. I just didn't know what to do right now, I was thinking I needed to find a way to get a pregnancy test. I mean, this could be a false alarm. I really hoped it was. Just then I got a knock on my door. It was my father letting me know we would be leaving in 30 minutes. I got up, jumped in the shower. I had already laid my things out that I was wearing.

The night went well. Jr. received award after award and dinner was awesome. I forgot my troubles for a while but once we returned home I was back to square one. I sneaked and called Shun to tell him that some way I needed a test just to be sure. I might have been scared and upset for nothing. But since I had been having my cycle. I'd never missed so I needed to be absolutely sure. I even had money saved from my allowance if I were to ever think about an abortion.

"I wouldn't dare think about putting that on my credit card, but since you already told your grandmother and she didn't believe in them that wouldn't work. At least let me buy that, I can ask my mom, she comes around once in a while. I told you we are in this together, maybe you don't believe me but I will never turn my back on you. I care for you and if we are having a baby I will love and care for the baby. I have had a very rough life without my father being there and my mother being addicted to drugs. She only comes around mostly when she has gotten pregnant and needing to unload another child. My grandmother is the best, she is really our mother, she never raises her voice at us or her daughter. She always prays for her and us and she always tells us she will be here for us until she takes her last breath. She asks my mother if she prays for herself. I made a vow that if I ever had children I would never abandon them. I had a plan for my life, I would graduate high school, then college, get myself established, get married, enjoy my wife a little while, then start a family, but sometimes things don't go as planned. I may have to get a better job and attend school at night. But please, believe me when I tell you I'm going to do all within my power not to have to depend on your parents. I will look for my mother, sometimes I see her standing on the corner. I will see you at school tomorrow. Don't stay up all night worrying, we are going to be just fine, you hear me?"

"Yes, thank you, I really feel like you mean what you are saying."

"I do. I love you, okay?"

"Okay, now goodnight."

"Goodnight."

I turned off the light and lay there thinking about my mother. She was the voice of the family. I didn't fear my father as much. I was sure he would come around. It seemed like forever before I drifted off to sleep. I got up at my usual time, got showered and dressed for school, just as I got in my car my cell phone rang. I looked at it, it was Shun calling.

"Good morning."

"Good morning to you. I was calling to let you know I found my mother. She got the test for me. I had to give her $10.00 to do it for me. That's sad but I did, so how do you want to do this?"

"I want to be very careful, I don't want to take a chance and get caught."

"Well, I have to work after school, you can come there. I will put it in a McDonald's bag and you can go into the bathroom

there, that way we will be together when you find out."
"Sounds like a plan to me, see you at school, thanks. Shun?"
"Yes?"
"I love you."
"I love you too. See you later."
Today seemed like the longest day of the year. I couldn't possibly stay for practice so I lied again. I headed straight to McDonald's, got the test, went into the bathroom, read the directions, took the test, almost fainted. I had to sit there for a minute to collect myself. I stayed in there so long, Shun sent one of the workers in to check on me. I came out finally and he was waiting for me, he was looking all excited, wondering what I was going to say. I couldn't say a word, I just burst into tears. He just held me and told me we were going to be alright. I sat down, felt like I had witnessed my first murder.

Shun asked, "Where do we go from here?"
"Just let me think a few days."
"Okay, well, if it's okay with you can I let my grandmother know that it's true? Since you can talk to her?"
"That will be fine."
"Would you like to speak to her before we sit down and talk to your parents?"
"I'm afraid to, what is she going to think of me?"
"She is not going to judge you or think bad of you, she will only encourage you to do the right thing. That's why I won't let you go through this alone. She has taught me well and instilled good teachings in all of us, even though I knew better than to have sex. It happened and I will live with my choice, so when you are ready we can face your parents, let me know how you want to do this, just be strong, we will get through this."

Beth said to Shun, "I have to admit, you make me feel so much better. But I never told you how my mother feels about the projects, she thinks that everyone that lives there is poor, they are on welfare, they don't go to school or will never graduate, have lots of babies, don't want to work and anything else negative that you can think of, and last but not least, not good enough to have contact with people like us."

"Wow is all I can say, why didn't you tell me that she feels this way?"

"I didn't want to hurt your feelings and besides, just because she thinks like that doesn't mean everybody else does, which is why I developed feelings for you, you were always kind to me, always clean, maybe not the top of the line in your clothes but nevertheless neat, you are always on the honor roll and not hanging out with some of the guys that stay in trouble."

"Beth, I've experienced a lot of things in my young life and I made a promise to make something of myself so I have to stay focused, besides I don't want my grandmother to do any unnecessary worrying. I am decent, I will always respect others and I demand to be respected, so before you leave do you mind if I walk you to your car so we can have a word of prayer?"

"Sure, but I really don't know how to pray."

"You don't?"

"No, that's not something we do at home."

"Well, I will teach you, that's odd, you live the life you live and never give thanks. Oh well, let's go, I have to start my shift."

He prayed for them and their situation, gave Beth a hug, and told her to call him when she got a chance.

9

CHAPTER 2

I just didn't want to go home right away so I drove to the park and sat there and tried to figure out a plan of action, wondering if there was anything else I could do other than face my mother, and what would Jr. think of me? After sitting for about an hour I decided to go on home. I parked, went inside, and was surprised to see Dad home so early. He hugged me, asked how was my day and how was practice. I said it was going well, looking forward to competitions.

"So you know, we have had to put in a lot of practice if we expect to win."

My dad looked at me and said, "You okay?"

I said, "I'm fine, why do you ask?"

"I was just wondering because there was a message on the phone from Coach Blaine, you have not been to practice in quite a while and she had been leaving messages for your mother and me to call, said she had spoken with you and for you to tell us to get in touch with her and that you promised to show up, said you had been dealing with teenage things, and just what are teenage things?"

I stuttered a little bit, trying to regain my composure. I was thinking I had time to sort things out, seemed like it was going to be sooner than later on then. I just burst into tears.

"Oh, Daddy, I am so sorry. I didn't mean to disappoint you and Mom, please, please don't disown me. I never intended to bring shame on our family."

"Beth, dear, what are you talking about, what have you done? Tell me what is wrong."

"Daddy, I'm pregnant, I'm so sorry, I know I've let you both down."

"Oh my God, oh my God, how could you have let this happen? Your mother and I had such great plans for you. Who is this guy? Is it one of our friends, is it Drake? I know he seems to always be watching you."

"No, Daddy, his name is Peshun."

"Peshun! That name sound like trouble. What is your mother going to say?"

"Please don't call her, can this wait until she is home to discuss this? I'm feeling sick right now, please, I need to go lie down later. I can go and pick Shun up and bring him so that you can talk to the both of us."

"Pick him up, why can't he drive over?"

"He doesn't have a car."

"Is it because he can't drive?"

"No, he can't afford one."

"Why doesn't his parents purchase him one?"

"His father is not in his life, his mother is on drugs and he is being raised by his grandmother, he and his six siblings."

"Oh, my goodness, and just where does he live? Wait, don't tell me, we'll just wait until your mother is home. This is too much for me to handle right now. I will send for you when she arrives."

"Thank you, Daddy."

After I reached my room I called Shun and told him what happened. I told him I was so afraid and he apologized profusely, said he wished he was here with me and that I shouldn't have to be going through this alone. He asked if he could try to get out to my house so that I wouldn't have to be alone with them.

I said, "No, not right now, I would have to handle this until I can convince my parents that you are a decent young man and that it doesn't matter where you live or your family situation, we love each other and we are sticking together, as you always say, we will get through this. You did mean that when you said that, didn't you?"

"Of course I did, you don't trust me?"

"I do but sometimes when things get tough young couples break up."

"Beth, you have my word, my solemn promise that I'll always be there for you and our child."

CHAPTER 3

I laid back on the bed with my hands folded behind my head, looking up toward the ceiling. I remembered Shun's prayer. I decided to try and pray and I repeated everything he had said and it seemed like instantly I began to feel better. Does prayer really work? I thought that I would do this often if this was what happened when you prayed. I felt so relaxed, I began to drift off to sleep. It felt like it had only been about 30 minutes that I had been asleep when I heard a knock on my door. It was Symie telling me my mother wanted to see me in her office. I looked at the clock, I had slept for two hours. I got up but before I left the room I looked up towards the ceiling and mouthed the words "Help, Lord."

CHAPTER 4

I walked into my mother's office. She and my father were sitting there, my mother had her head down and my father watched me. Looking all sad, he said, "Have a seat."

I spoke to my mother. She raised her head. "Your father says you have some news to tell me."

I took a deep breath. I looked from my father to her. "Yes, I'm pregnant."

"He told me that but I didn't believe him. I told him you had to tell me *even* though I still don't believe it, is this some kind of a joke? This can't be true, Beth, you are only 15 years old. How could you? What has gotten into you? Did someone rape you?"

"No."

"Are you covering up for someone?"

"No."

"Do you know who it is?"

"Yes."

"Where did we go wrong? You sure it wasn't Drake?"

"No, Mother, we are only friends. He likes me but that's not the way I feel about him."

"Well, then who is it? Wait, is he the reason you were late coming home and missing practice to be with him? I wondered why you looked at your phone and hurried out of the room."

"Yes."

"Oh, my goodness, who is he and where does he live, in our estates?"

"No, Mother. His name is Peshun, he is 16 years old, he is an honors student. He is *very* respectful. He lives with his grandmother and six siblings in the Zion Hills Housing Community. His father is not in his life and his mother is addicted to drugs."

My mom's eyes got as big as a basketball with tears streaming down her face. My father went over to comfort her.

"How could you, Beth? As if being pregnant isn't bad enough, you have gone against what I asked you not to do. Why didn't I notice anything?"

"Mother, you must remember, you are hardly *ever* home, you're *never* available when I have problems. I can always talk to Symie or Rosalita, but sometimes we need our parents."

"Oh, so now you are blaming me. Am I to blame for you being pregnant?"

"No, I'm just saying I only have myself to blame. Peshun has promised that he and I are in this together."

"Sure, if you think a lowlife from the projects will not abandon you, you better think again."

"He promised and I believe him."

CHAPTER 5

"Your father and I were discussing this God-awful situation that you have put us in. I know you have told Keana, haven't you?"

"Really, I thought you both told each other everything we do, I didn't know how to tell her this and besides, she still thinks I am a virgin. I didn't want her questioning me or trying to talk me out of having a relationship with Shun."

"Maybe it wouldn't have been a bad idea if you had told her, maybe she could have talked some sense into you. We have decided since only the four of us know, wait, did you tell Jr.?"

"No."

"Good, let's keep it that way. We are going to another state, can't have our name tarnished here."

"What about what we want? And besides, Shun told his grandmother and she doesn't believe in abortions. She is a God-fearing woman and they will not agree to this."

"Who are they to agree to anything?" said her mother. "They have nothing, no money, nothing, look at where they live. Oh,

Beth, how could you?"

"Dad, please, help me, just convince Mother to let me get Shun and his grandmother to come over and discuss this with them."

"No, no," her mother said, "never will I allow people like that to enter my home or be seen coming in here."

"They are good people and people."

"Nevertheless, they are not going to harm us or steal from us."

"How can you speak so badly about them?"

Dad said, "Listen, Elizabeth, even though our decision is final, let's talk to them and let them know our plans."

She hesitated a minute and said, "Like I said, they will not be allowed in our home, we will have to meet them out somewhere. Beth, you set up something so we can talk, let us know ahead of time so that I can arrange for someone to cover."

My dad said to let him know because he was done with court early most days and he might have to cancel meeting his buddies on the golf course one afternoon.

CHAPTER 6

Looking up at the ceiling, Beth mouthed, "Thank you, Lord, so by the time they meet up maybe they will have a change of heart about the abortion." Then she called Shun to let him know what just happened. She wouldn't dare tell him all that was said, just about them wanting her to get rid of the baby, and then the part about them setting up a meeting, then he asked Beth what she really wanted to do.

"I mean, I don't believe in them but I want you to be happy and want you to make the decision that you can live with, if you decide to go along with your parents I won't like it but I'll try and understand. Now if you decide to keep the baby, you won't regret it. So you tell me?"

"As I told you, we are not a praying family but the other day, I was so distraught lying on my bed I thought about you praying for us, so I repeated the same prayer and I felt better instantly, and I tried it again, I always feel better afterwards. I am beginning to believe that prayer works. I decided to do it often and said I will always do it."

I went up to my room to take a shower and get dressed for bed. I took a bubble bath and once in bed I had a very serious talk with God, about everything. I asked him to guide the situation. I said to him, "I know we are young, inexperienced, and don't know anything about being parents, but I know we love each other and I don't want to get rid of our baby," so I said, "Lord, what do we do?"
He actually spoke to me if there is such a thing as him speaking to you; I honestly thought I heard a voice. He said, "Do the right thing, everything you need to know will come naturally." It seemed like I could feel his presence. I said, "Thank you." So that was my final decision, we were going to be parents. God does see hear and answer prayers.
"I am so proud of you," my grandmother always said, "you can't go wrong when you trust God."

CHAPTER 7

So we set a date to meet Saturday afternoon. I would go get Shun and his grandmother and we would be meeting at a hotel in Buckhead far away from where we both lived. Saturday morning I called Shun to let him know I was on my way, and that I would be there in five minutes. He gave me the directions to their apartment. I called back to let him know I was outside. I didn't have a problem going inside, but we had a long way to go. Ms. Mattie and Shun came out. Once they were in the car, he introduced us. She reached over and gave me a hug, said she was glad to finally meet me.

"Shun talks about you all of the time, so what's going on, if I may ask?"

"My parents are very upset with me because they consider themselves as socialites and this is not only a disgrace to them, they are more worried about what their friends will say or think."

"Oh, I see."

"So I'm letting you know right now this is not going to be easy,

23

and it's really my mother who is call the shots, I can't make any promises about how this is going to turn out."

Ms. Mattie said, "Everything is going to be alright, Shun and I had prayer just before we walked out the door, well, is it okay if we pray again?"

"Sure, I don't know a lot about God and prayer but I've been trying it ever since Shun prayed for us."

"Well, baby, prayer is just your sincere thought and request to God, a conversation with him, my mother used to always say just a little talk with Jesus makes things okay. So would you like to lead us? If not I'm always willing."

"Okay, I'll try, I just hope I won't disappoint you."

"You won't."

So before we drove off Beth prayed a powerful prayer.

"I couldn't tell you don't know how."

"Thank you, I'm learning, one thing I have found out is that it relaxes me and makes me feel better. Where are we headed to?"

"Buckhead."

"Buckhead? Why so far? I have to be honest with you, my mother doesn't want to be where someone may notice her out with people so different from us."

"Oh, and what makes us different? I'm looking at you and you don't seem to be of another race, are your parents white or something else?"

"No, they are black."

"So what makes us different?"

"Well, you live in the projects. Shun does not have a car and he works at McDonald's."

"Oh, I get it, we are not good enough for your family?"

"To be honest, no, but I am not like my mother, we are all the same after I really got to know Shun, the way he carried himself and the way he treated me, I said my mother has this all wrong. I love Shun for the young man he is. I feel that I can trust everything he says and even though I'm young I can tell he is being raised right."

Ms. Mattie said, "I can certainly hold my own, I am not afraid of them."

CHAPTER 8

As we drove up to the hotel to valet park, Beth's parents were going inside. She said, "Those are my parents there."

We could only see the back of them.

"Very well groomed, look like they could buy the world if they wanted to, what does your parents do?"

"My father is a judge and my mother is a chief heart surgeon."

"Wow, well, here goes."

We got out of the car, got our ticket, walked inside, we had a top-floor suite. We caught the elevator up to the 25th floor. It opened up in the suite. Ms. Mattie and Shun had never seen anything like this. They were looking all around, my mother and father were standing there, she slightly elbowed my dad and rolled her eyes back like she couldn't believe that I would be involved with people like this.

"Mom, Dad, this is Peshun and his grandmother, Ms. Mattie."

Everyone smiled and reached out their hands, but my mother, she walked away saying, "Let's be seated for dinner and get this over with."

My father said, "How are you?"

My mother said, "I don't have all day."

We walked over to the elegantly set table and took our seats. "We only have 30 minutes to discuss this before dinner is served."

"30 minutes, Mother?"

"30 minutes, it's not going to take me long to say what I have to say."

"What about everyone else here?"

"What about them? Listen, I'll get straight to the point, my husband and I have agreed that Beth is not having this baby and so that all ties will be broken with the both of you we have agreed to pay you $100.00.00 to relocate to another state and the stipulation is never contact my daughter again."

"Mother, how could you say and do such a thing? Daddy, I know that this is not your idea, you are just going along with Mom."

"I, well, we talked about it."

"Well, I have something to say, I'm not having an abortion and I am not leaving Shun. I'm ashamed to say you are my parents. I have a say in the matter, if you try and force me I will move in with Shun or run away."

"How dare you! Calm down, child."

Shun said, "I have something to say."

Elizabeth said, "What could you possibly have to say that I even want to hear?"

Ms. Mattie stood up. "Now you hush up and listen."

She spoke so loud my parents immediately got quiet.

"Now you listen to me, I am a God-fearing woman, I've struggled all of my life to raise my children by myself, an unwed mother, and now I am raising my daughter's children. Yes, times are hard, always have been, but God is good to us. We never begged, borrowed, or stole from anybody, that's a lot of money and it sounds good but I wouldn't dare touch a cent of it. You not only want to murder their baby, you want to pay us to move out of town and not contact Beth anymore. What kind of people are you? I've never met anybody like you and I pray I never do. Listen, these are kids that made bad choices and they have decided to live with that. And I'm supporting them all the way. Both seem to be good kids doing good in school and you both seem to be highly educated fools, now you wait a minute, I'm not finished."

Mom sat back down.

"Now my grandson is an awesome young man, he has never given me any problems, makes straight A's in school, never been disrespectful or been in any trouble, always attends church, never misses a day of praying, so I thank God for him and I demand that we be treated with respect. Just because we live in the projects doesn't mean that we will just do anything, so you take that money and put it back in your purse because we can't be bought. Is this understood?"

They both nodded their heads.

"I'm sorry, Shun, I had to jump in there, is there something you would like to say?"

"I think enough has been said already, in fact I think too much has been said. Last but not least, I love Beth, if she will have me after all that has been said and done I will be a good father to my child and I certainly won't be raising my child to look down its nose at people who are less fortunate, as a matter of fact when we were coming in I was thinking my grandmother was going to have her first meal in an elegant upscale hotel that she is so deserving of that she can't afford. Enough has been said and done to ruin my appetite, so Beth, if you will I would like to leave now."

"Wait, please, can't we work something out?" said her mother.

"Everything has already been worked out and as you stated, Dr. Tirans, it would only take 30 minutes and you managed to screw it up in about 10 minutes, goodbye."

CHAPTER 9

They left Beth's parents sitting there, gave the valet a tip, and decided to stop by for fast food. Beth apologized for her parents' behavior.

Ms. Mattie said, "You are not responsible for them and you two will do just fine. Not what I expected from you, Shun, a baby at this age, but it is what it is. I expect all of your teachings to fall into place, understood?"

"Yes, Granny."

"Now Beth, I don't know anything about you, but you seem a lot different than your folks, so stay positive and with lots of prayers God can change things, you hear me?"

"Yes, ma'am."

"Now tell me about you, are there any siblings?"

"Yes, I have one brother, he just graduated from high school and he's headed off to college."

"What does he have to say about this?"

"I haven't told him yet even though I'm sure he knows, my parents may have told him and he's waiting for me to tell him, I am

a little afraid of what he's going to say or think of me. Mom and
Dad had high hopes for the both of us. Even though they are
hardly ever around doesn't show much love and concern for us,
I mean I'm sure they love us, but since their lives are so busy
they try and make up for it with things. They pretty much want
us to succeed and do everything on our own."
So we ended the day with Shun and I working on a plan for our
child.

CHAPTER 10

Once I returned home Mom and Dad were sitting there
waiting for me.

Mom said, "May we have a word with you?"

"Please, I don't want to do this anymore."

"Just a few minutes."

I gave in, sat down.

"Listen, Beth."

Beth interrupted her mother.

"Dad, you are supposed to be the head of this home, yet
you never stand up. You go along with Mom letting her run
everything even though you know sometimes she is wrong
and what she did today was just about unforgivable, but I
feel if she had known better she would have done better.
What makes you think that money solves all problems? I
would take us being a family any day over money. Mom, the
money your parents left you and the money the two of you
make has ruined our family as far as I'm concerned. Fur-
thermore, I don't care to discuss this or hear what else you

have to say. Like I stated earlier, I am keeping the baby and Shun and Ms. Mattie can't be bought, so use the money to purchase more property or whatever you choose to do with it. But I'm done."

CHAPTER 11

I went into my room and closed the door. As soon as I sat on my bed there was a knock on my door.

"Yes?"

"It's me, Jr., can I come in?"

"Yes, hey, what's up? Haven't seen much of you lately."

"Same here, I know I've been out a lot lately just getting out of school, I've been hanging out with the boys, time goes by so fast, we will be off to school before you know it."

"I have something to tell you, here, sit down beside me."

"What's wrong?"

"Jr., I know that I can talk to you and I apologize for not coming to you. First of all, has Mom and Dad told you anything about me?"

"No, I really thought that was why you came to my room."

"Well, I need to tell you that I am pregnant."

"You are what?"

"I'm pregnant."

"Are you sure? I mean, I don't know what to say, why haven't you said something before now? So Mom and Dad know, which is why you asked the question earlier."

"Yes, they do, I didn't want to bother you because you were getting preparing for graduation and I didn't want anything to interfere with your excitement."

"To be honest, I never would have guessed you were not a virgin, wow, who's the father, Drake?"

"We are only friends, that's all I've ever wanted from him."

"Well, who is he?"

"His name is Peshun and he's from school, he lives in the projects."

"Oh, my goodness, I bet Mom had a fit."

"You cannot even imagine, not only that, she is trying to make me have an abortion and tried to pay Shun and his grandmother off, offered them some money to go away and not contact me ever."

"Are you being serious?"

"Yes, but I want you to know that I am keeping the baby and I will finish school and go on to college."

"I'm almost speechless, I know that this is a lot for you to handle right now, of course I am shocked. I'm numb, I don't know how to feel or what to say, I'm not going to come down on you or turn my back on you. It seems you have worked things out for yourself, I still love you, always have, always will. I'm here for you, you seem so calm about this."

"I am now, I'm learning how to pray and trust God."

"Oh, where is this coming from? We never pray, read the Bible, or go to church."

"Shun and his family do all of that, they trust God to lead and guide their lives."

"Sounds pretty deep. We have to talk about this some more, I'm glad you told me before Mom did even though I'm not going to mention that we talked, then she will tell me in her own way so keep your chin up. I have to run now, I'm fifteen minutes late meeting the boys. I love you."

CHAPTER 12

Beth prayed and turned in for the night. The next morning Beth went to Symie to tell her everything. She was upset but then asked her if there was anything she could do for her.

She said, "As a matter of fact there is."

She asked if she would speak to her mother about a doctor's appointment and wanted to know if she would go with her.

"You sure you don't want to discuss this with your mother yourself?"

"No, I don't want to get into a confrontation with her, but I need to see a doctor. I will have a talk with her later, now is not the time."

Once Beth left and her mom came in the room, where she was getting ready to leave for rounds at the hospital, Symie asked if she had a minute.

"What is it?"

"I told her Beth came to me this morning and told me what was going on, to be honest I don't want to be in the middle of this. I asked her if there was anything I could do, she asked me to see if you would make an appointment for her to see a doctor and told me she wants me to go with her."

"She asked you to go?"

"Yes, she says she doesn't want any problems with you and I have always taken her to her for her visits. So I was hoping that it would be okay."

"Well, I guess I don't have a choice right now, she is thinking that I am one of the worst mothers in the world right now. I was going to try and reason with her again, I don't know what to do, however I will make the appointment in another county in case she changes her mind, wouldn't want this to get out."

"Yes, ma'am."

Beth was about to go to her first class when she saw Shun, he gave her a peck on the cheek.

"What's up?"

"I'm trying to see the doctor so I can find out what I need to do. I asked Symie, the lady that works for us, to work things out with my mother to get me in to see a doctor, and I asked her to go with me. I really don't want my mother to do anything right now."

"Do you think she will go along with that?"

"She will, if she fights me on this I'll let her know that I will run away, and I want you to come along with us."

"I was hoping you would let me. I would love to go at least to as many visits as I can, especially your first one. Well, I have to run now, we are both late."

When she sat down KeKe passed her a note, wanting to know why she hadn't called or returned her calls and that she missed hanging out. She sent her a note back saying she was sorry and that she had been taking care of some very important business and would get with her as soon as possible and explain things. "So please be patient, I miss you too."

Once Beth came home Symie told her she was coming up to her room in a minute to speak to her. She went to her room, set her things down, and laid on the bed, uttered her now favorite words, "Lord, help."

CHAPTER 13

A few minutes later Symie was at the door, she came in and sat down beside me.

"Your mother wasn't happy but she agreed since everyone is under so much stress, she won't press the issue, she will only do it if you go to another county for your visits."

"Why is that?"

"She said just in case you change your mind about having the baby."

"Not a chance, my mind's made up and I am keeping my baby. In fact, I'm getting excited, I know you will be here for me, won't you?"

"Yes you that already with you and Shun's grandmother teaching us things, I know that it will all work out."

"When's the appointment?"

"It's on Saturday, she didn't want you missing school."

"Good, Shun wants to be there for this special occasion, maybe he can make most of them."

"It's 11:30."

"Okay, I will let him know so he can make sure he can get off from work. Thank you for your love and kindness you've shown all of our lives. I hope you are not upset with me, I really care about what you think of me. I know that you love us and want what's best for us, you have been more like a mother to us and we appreciate you. To be exact, you've been more of a mother to me than my mother has, she has always put her career first and just left us kids to the staff. Well, I guess better you all staying all these years than others coming and going. I love you."

"I love you too, dear, we'll get through this."

"Thank you."

Symie got up to leave. "I'll see you when you come down to dinner."

I called Shun to let him know about the plans for Saturday and that it was in the next town.

"Your mother really doesn't want anyone to know it."

"It's not going to be a secret much longer but we will see how things go."

"I'm glad you let me know in enough time to change my schedule for that day, we usually work for each other when one of us has something to do good, okay, I will talk to you later."

When I went down to dinner, Dad was at the table. Mom hadn't made it home yet.

Dad smiled. "How are you, princess?"

I looked at him. I always felt that he loved me when he called me that. "I'm fine, Dad, how are you?"

"I'm good. Listen, I'm sorry about all that has gone on and it made me feel awful when you said I'm supposed to be the head of this house and yet I let your mother run things. I thought about it long and hard and I had a talk with her to let her know

44

things have to change, we have to work together and that I would no longer sit back and let run things. She put up a fight but I put my foot down so she agreed, so things are going to be different."

"You sure about that?"

"I'm sure."

"Great."

"So are you positive about your plans and staying with Shun?"

"I am."

"Well, we will support you, now you have to work on a plan with your schooling, do you still plan to attend college?"

"Yes, Dad, nothing is changing except I will be a mother."

"Give me a little time to work on your mother, change is not going to happen overnight, trust me, it will happen."

"Thanks, Dad, I knew I could count on you."

"You're always going to be my lil' princess and I love you."

"I love you too. Listen, Dad, I know I let you and Mom down but I promise to still make you and Mom proud of me."

"I'm going to hold you to that."

CHAPTER 14

I woke up early on Saturday. I was so anxious about the visit. By 8:30 I was done getting dressed, I had breakfast and I was waiting for Symie. She knocked on my door to see if I was ready to leave.

I said, "I've been ready for so long, it seems like I got dressed yesterday."

She laughed and we went out to the car. She wanted to know if I wanted Jeffrey to drive us or if we would drive ourselves.

"Jeffrey is our driver, if we go out as a family or if Mom and Dad don't feel like driving he will."

I decided to take my car and that she would drive, I called Shun, he was already dressed and waiting, I told him we would be there in 20 minutes, we already left home. We picked Shun up. I introduced the two of them. Symie said, "He is handsome." We laughed and talked all the way to the doctor. We went inside, filled out all of the paperwork, I had already gotten enough money to cover things but my dad gave Symie the insurance card, I'd just deposit my money back in the bank. I was called to the back, got undressed. Symie helped me, then left and let Shun come in.

After the nurse took my vitals she asked me some questions, she left and came back with the doctor, his name was Dr. Rancifer.

He introduced himself to us and since I was so young, he explained everything to us that he was doing to examine me, and Shun held my hand the entire time.

When he was done he said, "Well, what do you want, a boy or a girl?"

Shun and I hugged and said, "Whichever one God blesses us with, as long as the baby is healthy."

The test came up showing I was a little over three months, and he wanted me to come back in two weeks for an ultrasound. We looked at each other, then he explained what an ultrasound was.

He gave me some vitamins and told me to take one every day, also letting me know their importance. He was so kind and patient with us being that we were young and knew nothing about being parents. I got dressed and went back to the waiting room and hugged Symie. She was excited too, we decided to have lunch and found somewhere close by. We talked and ate, I told Shun about the conversation I had with my dad, and that he was supporting us, it made him happy. I told him we had to make some decisions about our schooling and our plans for being parents.

"Sure, we will talk, but we have lots to discuss before we finalize our plans, do you agree?"

"I agree."

"Good, then my next day off we will get together."

They took Shun home since it was a little while before he had to be at work. They all went inside. Beth wanted Symie to meet

Ms. Mattie and to tell her the news. Once inside they could not believe how clean and nice their apartment was, plus they got to meet all of his siblings. The visit was good and Ms. Mattie invited them to church the next morning. Symie looked surprised but she agreed to go. Once we made it home Mom and Dad were in the sunroom having lunch, Mom with a strange look on her face.

Dad was all smiles. "Well, how did things go, princess?"

"Well, Daddy, you are going to be a grand poppy. I'm a little over three months."

Mom said, "You sure you want—"

Dad cut her off. "Lizabeth."

"Yes?"

He gave her a look, then she said, "Great," and left the room. "We will get through this like I said, just give your mother a little time and space, please understand she will not change overnight, okay? Have you had lunch?"

"Yes, we ate in town."

"Good, well, I'm going up to take a nap."

"Go right ahead, I'll see you in a bit."

I went upstairs, took another shower, got in bed under the covers, and mouthed, "Thank you, Lord."

CHAPTER 15

The next morning Symie and I got dressed and made it to Shun's. He rode with us and everyone else rode the church bus, they all looked real nice in their Sunday best. We were early enough to all sit together. Ms. Mattie sang in the choir and boy, did she have a beautiful voice, and the sermon was awesome: "Just trust God." I got into it and enjoyed every minute of it.

Symie said she hadn't thought about church in quite some time but that was changing, and that sermon just confirmed for me for sure everything was definitely going to be alright. The pastor asked if anyone wanted prayer. We got up at the same time, even Shun went down. We held hands while he prayed. We left and Ms. Mattie told us she had prepared dinner and asked if we would join them. We said we would love to.

We sat down to a wonderful meal, she certainly could cook. After we left we discussed the service, the preacher, Ms. Mattie, and all of the kids, how well mannered they were and they were such a close family. They might not have much but to me they had everything that made a family a family, they could teach my family a thing or two. We made it home. I went to my room, Symie went to check on things. I had purchased a Bible for the service today so after I showered again I decided to sit up in bed and thumb through it. I glanced at a couple of chapters in Genesis, then I looked in the back and saw where I could look up certain reference words and the first one I wanted to look up was faith. I really wanted to understand what it meant to have faith and also what it meant to believe, after a while my eyes got heavy, but before I drifted off to sleep I said, "Thank you, Lord."

So Monday morning, I got dressed for school. I was thinking about what I was going to tell Coach Blaine because I was dropping off the squad. I thought I would tell her I was having some family issues and that I really couldn't focus or give this my all right now, and I asked KeKe if I could give her a ride home this evening so we could talk. She said okay. The coach was a little upset, said I was one of her best girls. I apologized and asked her to please understand, she finally said she understood. We left school and drove to my favorite thinking spot, KeKe and I got out and walked the trail. I told her everything, she was shocked, I explained that I was going to finish school and go on to college. She now understood why I had been so distant because I had a lot on my mind. I asked her to please not tell anyone right now until Shun and I had worked things out. We were going to talk more over the weekend and we would continue to until our plan was all the way in place. I told her that I loved her and didn't want to lose her as my best friend; she said that was not going to happen. I dropped her off, headed home to work on some plans for the meeting with Shun, and I asked him to have a list of things too. Then we would sit down with my parents and his grandmother.

CHAPTER 16

Mom was still a little silent and standoffish. I had come to realize that with much prayer she would come around, I couldn't be made to feel any worse than I already felt by making such a foolish mistake, but I believed that God had forgiven me and we were going to make it through this. I might even be a little stronger in the end. Dad told me to let him know when we were ready to talk, he didn't want me to be stressed, I told him thanks and we would talk real soon.

CHAPTER 17

Shun made sure he had the whole day off on Saturday just so they could go over each other's plans with a fine-tooth comb and to see what needed to be worked out to meet each other's needs, so after picking him up at noon the went to the library to go over things there. As usual they had prayer before going inside, this always made the situation better, it was so calming and relaxing. They went to the last table so they would be away from everyone else. Shun stated that he was always taught that ladies go first but in this case he wanted whatever made her feel comfortable.

She said, "Thank you for the offer but I want you to go first."
"If that will please you, my dear, here goes," and he took out his list. "If you are unhappy with anything I'm saying please know that things can be changed, now since your mother thinks so low of me, my family, and where we live—"
"Please, if I may interrupt right now, it's about the three of us, you, me, and our baby."
"I know, but I also want to change her mind about some things."

"Go ahead."

"Now I am going to finish school, I am in the process of looking for a better job, and depending on the job I get I may have to go to college part time at first, but as time goes on I may be able to take a full load, my grandmother and my sisters have agreed to help out with the baby if you will allow this. I know it's not going to be okay with your mother but we'll see. Now I know there's not a lot of money on my end, but I have been saving all that I can and I have been taking on as many hours as I can just so I will be able to help out. I'm going to go above and beyond to be the young man that I am being raised to be."

"Thank you again."

"You don't have to thank me, we are in this together, as I've always told you. There's more that I have written down but I'm anxious to hear some of your plans."

"As far as I'm concerned you have said enough and I'm pleased, now I was undecided about continuing at school or changing to attend girls' school, just until I have the baby, I really don't want to leave school but I also don't want to embarrass my family or you."

"Beth, I'm not the least bit embarrassed, you forgot I'm the other half of this. I would love for you to stay at school with me, that way I can watch you and be right there with you."

"You are so nice to me but what about your mother? Remember, you are only fifteen."

"My father said he would take care of her, told me no matter what he's not turning his back on me. So when we have our family meeting it will be discussed, so the decision between the two of us, we will be in school together, now I have more time to really focus on my schoolwork. My grades are good, I too am going to finish college even though I don't have to work, and I've saved quite a bit of money and I will continue to, I'm not going to tell you that I don't have to save any money because I want you to be happy with your choices. I would love for the baby to spend lots of time with your family, that's awesome," Shun said, "now I have something to tell you as well as ask you."

"Yes?"

"I've never had anyone to teach me how to drive, much less anything to drive, so I want to know at some point will you teach me how?"

"Well, I never thought you did know how given your upbring-ing, please don't take this the wrong way and also since I am only fifteen maybe not me but I will make sure you get your li-cense, I'll speak to Symie."

"Okay."

"One more thing," Beth said, "was if it's okay I would love to keep going to your church and a little bit later get involved with some activities."

"I would like nothing better."

"So we have school and your job situated worked out right now, that's a load off my shoulders, we will work out more things as time goes on. I will let you know more about the meeting, I do know that it will be next Saturday. I will call you about the time as soon as we work that out."

"Sounds good to me, let's say a prayer and get some lunch."

"Sure, I've been craving hot wings," Shun said."

"I know just the place."

CHAPTER 18

Once they received their order they sat down. Beth couldn't believe how smooth things were going thus far. She told him she couldn't be happier with her choice in a boyfriend. He said he felt the same. After lunch Beth dropped Shun off and went home. Her parents were in the sunroom having a discussion and a glass of wine. Dad asked how my day had gone. I almost didn't want to talk in front of my mother but did, so instead I told him I had been with Shun and we had gone over some things and we were ready to have the family meeting. I let him know that next Saturday was the day, would we be here? Her mother hadn't said a word until then.

"No, I mean we can meet somewhere where dinner can be served, we knew that wasn't true because dinner can be served here, but anyway, okay, Mother," she added, "since we didn't get to have dinner the last time we can go back there, we knew she still didn't want to be seen out with them, we will meet there at 1:00. I'll talk to you later, I need to find Symie."
I found her upstairs in the hallway, we gave each other a hug,

she asked me what was going on. I told her about the meeting and about Shun wanting to learn how to drive. She said she would take care of it, she would let Jeffrey use her personal car to teach him. He owed her a big favor and that way she wouldn't run into any problems with her parents, especially her mother. Beth gave her another hug and thanked her, she also told her it would be a secret.

"I can't thank you enough. I'm a little tired, I'm going to my room."

Before they went their separate ways, Beth reminded her of her next appointment in two weeks. She assured her that she hadn't forgotten, she had marked it on her calendar. She thanked her for loving her all these years.

CHAPTER 19

Saturday morning Beth woke up bright and early. Before she got out of bed, she said a prayer thanking God for things thus far and for the meeting that was about to take place today, that it would be decent and in order. She took her shower and went down for breakfast. She and Symie were alone in the kitchen. She let Beth know that she overheard her mother inviting Jr. to the meeting to see what kind of people she had gotten herself involved with and that maybe he could persuade her to make other arrangements after the meeting and let it be a surprise when he showed up, she stated that she loved her brother and she respected his opinion and at this point she would appreciate him respecting hers.

"So I'll let you know how things go, just know that I love you and I'm here for you."

"Thanks."

CHAPTER 20

Beth picked up her crew. Little did she know that Shun's mother was also with them. Her name was Mi'lan. She had come by the house the other day and her mother told her what was going on and that she was going to be a grandmother. She was so happy and excited, she said she was going to clean up her act and be a good grandmother like her mother had been to her children all of these years. She thanked her mother for all she had done to raise her children while she had been out in the streets doing her own thing, drugs and everything else you can imagine. She asked if she could attend the meeting, they said yes even though they didn't expect her to show up, she always told lies and broke promises but she was there and had cleaned up the best she could because all those years of drug use had taken a toll on her looks. So Beth was *very* shocked and surprised to meet her and was glad she came along. She had to make sure they prayed before they drove off and believe it or not Mi'lan asked to lead the prayer. She asked God to forgive her for the way she had been living her life. She asked him to forgive her for abandoning her children. She asked her and she asked her mother to forgive her for having to take care of her children for so long and she asked God for strength to stay clean and sober.

"I know it's not going to be easy but I know that I can do all things through you that strengthens me so that I can be a good grandmother to my first grandchild and that all will go well with this meeting, and please help me to hold my tongue if things start to get out of hand because I look for any reason to get started and I know you know that I can do some cutting up, Amen." She said to her mother and Shun, "I know I've made and broke a lot of promises before but I promise that things are about to change." The mere thought of being a grandmother made her look forward for a change.

CHAPTER 21

They made it to the hotel and went inside. They wondered why there were three people instead of two.
Beth acted surprised and said, "Jr., I didn't know you were coming," and she introduced him.

Her mother was standing there looking surprised to see this straggly looking woman, then Shun introduced her as his mother. Beth didn't know she was coming but after she showed up at the house she was allowed to come, why not? Everyone shook hands but, of course, her mother acted as if she was busy. She probably thought something was going to rub off on her.

They all walked over to the sitting area to talk before dinner was to be served. After they all were seated Beth's father started things off. He had been doing a great job of running the household. Beth was *very* proud of him.

"Now first let me apologize for the way things went at the first meeting, and let's please respect each other and listen to everyone that has something to say, is that understood?"

Everyone said yes except her mother.

"Elizabeth, is that understood?"

She half nodded yes.

"Very well, now the topic is open for discussion."

Beth and Shun were to get together and work out their plans for completing their education and for the baby.

"So we are going to hear them out before we speak."

Beth started but was cut off by Shun.

"Beth, allow me since I and my family are considered the underdogs here."

She sat back down in her seat. Shun decided to stand up.

"As I stated, I had a rough life with my father being absent and my mother being on drugs and barely around, but my grandmother stepped up and took us all in to keep us from being separated and in the system. She turned what looked like a hopeless situation into a positive upbringing; she also instilled good morals and values in each of us. She talked to us about sex and pregnancy, so it's not like I didn't know better, but on the other hand since I chose to step out of bounds with my teachings, I am going to accept responsibility and deal with this. We are going to raise our baby to the best of our ability, we are not asking you to do everything since we are young and inexperienced but we are asking you to stick by us. It has never occurred to us to abort, we are staying in school together, we discussed her leaving and returning once she had the baby but I asked her to stay there with me so that I could watch her. I've taken on more hours and I am looking for a better job. I am going on to college, once I graduate I won't be taking a full course load right away but I can assure you that we both will complete our education. My grandmother and my sisters had agreed to help with the baby and now my

mother. Now I don't have lots of money but I'm saving all
that I can to do my part so you all don't have to worry about
me running off or depending on the two of you, I'm asking
that you please give me a chance and please trust me, I'm not
going to disappoint myself or any of you, thank you." Shun
took his seat.

Beth said, "That pretty much sums up our plans, we don't know
a thing about being parents and we would really appreciate everyone's support, that's all I have to say."

Beth's father said that was very well spoken and that he could
feel the sincerity in his voice and felt that he meant everything
he said.

Ms. Mattie spoke and said, "The only thing she has to say is she
is going to support them in every way."

Mi'lan wanted to speak, she again stated that she was all excited, she said she knew she had to earn their trust. She said she
hadn't used drugs since she found out about the baby, she said
she knew it was not going to be easy but the baby was worth
her fighting for. Beth's mother finally said she didn't like the
fact that Beth chose to stay at school and that the least she
could do was go to the other school until she had the baby.
Beth told her, "I am staying at my school," and that she could
disown her if she couldn't deal with it.

Then Jr. wanted to speak. He said he was asked to attend the
meeting by his mother to try and persuade Beth to do other-
wise. Their father gave her a stern look. She sat back in her
chair.

"I'm sorry, Mother, to be saying this, but after listening to Shun
I have to support them. They seem to have worked things out. I
know that they are young but let's rally around them. They

made the decision to be mature about this, let's not make things more difficult for them. So I'm on board, Beth."

Beth got up and hugged her brother with tears in her eyes.

"Thank you."

He kissed her and told her he loved her.

Elizabeth thought to herself, *I've lost on every hand, these lowlifes are winning.*

CHAPTER 22

After all was said and done, everyone moved to the table for
dinner. It was an awesome meal, they all enjoyed it, but
Elizabeth only had a glass of wine. Once dinner was over with they
all finished their desserts, said their goodbyes, and left.

On the ride home Shun said, "That went better than the last time."
Mi'lan said, "I don't think your mother is too happy about this,
you think she is going to come around?"

"I pray she will eventually," my father said, "give her some
time, I know she feels that things are backfiring on her. She
thought Jr. was going to go along with her. Well, it's not too
much I can say right now, I have my own work cut out for me
right now so I need your prayers and your support. I'm going
into rehab for 30 days. If I feel I need more time I have the op-
tion to stay longer, we'll all be here for you, thanks."

Ms. Mattie asked Beth if she was coming to church tomorrow.
She said, "Of course, Symie and I will be there."

Mi'lan said, "Don't leave me out."

They were all shocked, they couldn't remember the last time

she was in church. Then she asked her mother if she could help with dinner.

"Sure, it seems like things just might be changing," but they had to be patient. She had done everything under the sun not to be trusted but they were willing to let her earn their trust again.

CHAPTER 23

Once again it was time for Beth to return for her appointment. This time she was having an ultrasound. They arrived, she was both scared and a little nervous. She mouthed her famous words, "Help, Lord." She didn't know what to expect when the procedure was underway. She saw the baby's heartbeat. She calmed down and was so excited, she found out that she was close to four months. My, how time flies. She and the baby were fine, maybe her next visit or two we would find out the sex, couldn't tell this time

The doctor said, "I always ask the question, what would you do if you had twins?"

"Are we having twins?"

"I didn't say that, I said I always like to ask the question."
She got dressed, got her instructions and the next appointment, and were off. They stopped again for hot wings, then they told Symie how everything went, including the question they were asked, no one was aware of twins and Beth didn't want to think about the possibility of twins.

"Let's change the subject."

They finished, then dropped Shun off. Beth expressed to Shun that she wasn't sure if she felt up to going to church in the morning but she hoped so because she knew she would be missing a few Sundays. Symie asked Beth how she was feeling.

And she said, "My life is about to change forever, it didn't really sink in until after the ultrasound. Will you explain to me all that will go on in the next five months?"

"Sure, but I don't want no problems with your mother thinking I'm overstepping my bounds."

"This will be between the two of us, she doesn't seem interested me or the baby's wellbeing, and at this point I don't want to discuss anything with her."

She agreed to give me a diary with important info, and also I could write notes to remember this time in my life.

CHAPTER 24

Dad and I made it home at the same time and he asked how I was and what had gone on today. I told him all of the day's events, even the question asked, and he couldn't recall anyone in either of the families with twins but that didn't mean there weren't any.

"Please don't mention that part to Mom right now. He didn't say for sure, just said he liked to ask the question. I'm sure if it were so he would have told me."

"So things haven't started to come around for you and your mom yet, have they?"

"No, she is not warming up yet, you said give her some time and I'm giving her space and besides, I don't want to be getting upset now so let's leave well enough alone now."

He hugged her and they walked inside. Mom wasn't home yet, she wasn't sure when she would make it home.

"Good, and I can keep it moving, go to my room, shower, and relax."

Jr. wasn't home either.

"I hardly ever see him."

As soon as I put my purse down KeKe called, wanting to know if I wanted to catch a movie. I told her of all the day's events and that I was tired, she said she loved me and please don't shut her out of my life. I promised that wasn't the case. And that I loved her too and we would get together real soon, in fact I wanted her to come over and spend the night, whatever night she chose.

"Good deal, I will call and let you know, love you."

"Love you more, bye."

I laid back on the bed and said a prayer, and the next thing I knew it was 11:00 at night. I had dozed off before I took my bath, I decided to take a bubble bath and just lay back, soak, and relax. I took a long look back into my young life and the changes that were taking place. I looked at the good life I'd always been able to live and the baby that was coming, and things were going to change with a child. I thought about my mother and if there would be any changes in her. We had so many things yet it didn't seem as though we had the things I felt that made Shun's family a family, that was love and togetherness. I would trade all the luxuries for the closeness. His motto was "The family that prays stays." Once I finished I laid down and watched television for about an hour. I thanked God and picked up where I left off.

CHAPTER 25

The next morning at breakfast the whole family was present when Dr. Tirans made an announcement.

They made it to the hotel and went inside, once inside they were surprised to see three people instead of two. Beth acted shocked and said "Jr. I didn't know you were coming" and she introduced him to Shun and his family.

"I'd like to speak for a moment, if I may. I'd like to apologize for my attitude and actions. I was a little devastated at the news of Beth's pregnancy, you are my baby and the last thing I expected was for you to get pregnant at your age and before you were married. I had to do a lot of thinking and I decided that I will be here for you, so I hope you can find it in your heart to forgive me," and she began to cry.

Everyone was so moved at the change in her.

Beth's father said, "I told you to give her some time and that she would come around."

They all hugged and were so excited they returned to their seats to finish their food. If they only knew she had another trick up her sleeve. She had someone to find Mi'lan and tried to bribe her with $10,000 dollars to break up her son and Beth so she could convince her that he was no good and to show her that he wouldn't be there for her, then she could have the baby aborted before it was too late.

Mi'lan met with her in private, took the money, and thought about how much crack she could smoke and enjoy herself for days. She thought to herself, *Aafter all the drugs are gone, I'm gonna quit and sober up for good.* She also promised not to mention any of this to anyone, and once the mission was complete, including the baby being gone, Elizabeth would give her a bonus when she received the other money being as though she would be done with rehab by then.

She had never had that much money, and if she had it, it would have gone up in smoke as per usual. She probably wouldn't even remember having it. She paced back and forth for days, trying to talk herself out of going back on her word. Her kids' faces kept flashing in her eyes, how happy they seemed to be because she was in their lives, always asking if she was coming back every time she walked out the door, no matter when she came back they always seemed to be waiting for her.

There was a corner store right before the crack house and she went into the store, went straight into the bathroom, and fell on her knees and started to pray. "Dear God, if you hear me, please help me to turn around and not go in the direction of that crack house. I'm begging you, if you keep me away this one time I promise I'll never go back."

CHAPTER 26

It was time again for Beth's visit to the doctor. She was a little disappointed that Shun couldn't go this time. The young man that usually covered for him had lost his father and they were shorthanded, plus he needed to get as many hours as he could even though he wanted to be there with her. He was sorry but he just couldn't make it. He asked if she would cancel and go next week, but she just went on and kept the one she had because something could come up next week and she wanted to keep every one of them if at all possible. So Symie was there with her and found out the news, it was twins after all. They were elated but shocked, not too much.

So because of the question the doctor asked, he said, "When I see there are two and the couple doesn't know and are really young like you are, I like to give them something to think about and then I reveal it on the next visit."

"Oh my God, I really wish Shun was here to share the news. He asked me to call him right away as soon as I found out but I'm not going to call him. I'm going to his job, let's stop and buy something that I can give him so he can guess, oh my God is all I can say. What's a good way to let the others know? I am a little over five months now, time is going so fast, no one is making fun of me at school and I couldn't ask for things to be any better. Shun is so wonderful in my life, if I had to do things over again but a little differently I would still choose to be with him."

We stopped at the mall and bought two blankets, blue and pink, two bottles same color, and put them in a gift bag, along with two cards saying "We love you, Daddy," a boy for him and a girl for me, two babies for the both of us. Thank you, God.

After dropping Symie off I couldn't get to him fast enough. He was so excited to see me. I sat down and as soon as he got a break he came over.

"Tell me, tell me!"

She gave him the bags, he saw the pink and the blue, then he took the contents out and said, "Does this mean what I think it means?"

"Yes, we really are having twins."

"I really have to work longer and harder and get my education because I am going to be the best father in the world!" Then he gave her a big kiss.

They sat there a minute until it got busy.

"Well, I have to get back to work, let me walk you to the car first. Can we say a quick prayer?"

"Always, thank you, dear God, for blessing us twice."

They both laughed.

CHAPTER 27

When Mi'lan knew anything she was back at home in her bed and all she could say was "Thank you, Lord, for hearing and answering my prayer." She was so grateful to him for not letting her go and get high. She had to check into rehab on Monday so he saved her from herself. She had hid the money, she just had to figure out a time and a place to return it. It was Sunday. Jr. was home and wanted to go to church with them since it seemed like they were really enjoying themselves. That was all they talked about when they came home, but this time Symie and Beth had asked them not to cook because they had dinner prepared every Sunday since they had been going with them, so they took everyone out to dinner. Ms. Mattie said that it would be too expensive to feed all of them, they told her not to worry, it was not a problem. They had to go in different cars to have enough room. Mi'lan was still thanking God and asking him for strength because she promised that she was keeping her word to God this time but also how to fix Elizabeth for good.

"I am returning all of her money, she thinks I am working on her little dirty deed."

After they returned home Jr. was now excited about the service and said if they didn't mind he wanted to go back every time he was home.

CHAPTER 28

All was well and things were running smoothly and Elizabeth seemed to be supporting the kids. She seemed happier, she was just wondering why Beth and Shun were still together and why she couldn't get in touch with Mi'lan. She told her not to call her phone and that she would be contacting her to see what she had accomplished. It didn't seem like anything, she hadn't spoken to her since that first meeting and her person hadn't seen her around for a minute. He really didn't want to ask anyone because he didn't know what this was about and he did not want to be involved in anything since he was on paper. She offered him more money but he was not willing to risk going back to jail for anybody, he didn't know if she was missing because she was dead or in jail, that was enough for him. So now she had to wait even though she figured she had just supplied her with some getting high money and she was furious to think that she had taken off with her money but she couldn't let her anger show and besides, Beth had gotten a lot bigger.

"Oh well, but I won't dare ask how many months exactly she is.

I can guess that my time to get things done has passed and it's already too late. I just have to cut my losses and move on. I certainly can't confront her. If I ever see her again, wouldn't want my family to know that I tried and once again failed. Well, you win some and you lose some. I can admit defeat on this one too. I gave it my best shot. I did the best I could to keep the projects out of our lifestyle, it never should have happened and I will never accept it."

CHAPTER 29

Mi'lan was 30 days into treatment and she was doing well. She didn't feel that she needed to continue. She was going to get a weekend pass just to test herself and they were having a coming-home party for her, and since Beth didn't want a shower she asked her if they could all bring gifts for the babies. She gave in and agreed, it was a really nice gathering, lots of their family and friends, and Mi'lan invited a lot of the people she had met in treatment that had graduated from the program. Even the director said she had done very well, she said she was motivated mostly by her children and especially the unborn twins. She knew she had to fight with every fiber of her being. She never wanted anything as much as she wanted to be drug free and a life change. It was well worth the fight. Unbeknownst to Beth, Shun and Jr. got together and invited some of their cousins and some of her friends. Jr. had asked their mother to ride with him somewhere since she had come home from the hospital early. She said she was tired but he in-sisted, her father and Symie had already left home, they knew where they were going but Elizabeth didn't. The hall was owned by one of Ms. Mattie's nephews. It was nice but still in the hood, so when Elizabeth arrived she was looking all around like she didn't belong there. She walked inside and looked around, saw all of the people and thought, *What is going on, is this a party/shower?*

When she saw all of the gifts and baby things, then she looked at this strange woman that looked like Mi'lan but much better. Maybe it was her sister. She was well groomed and had a little more weight on her. I was thinking, why wouldn't he tell me where we were going? I could answer that myself; he knew I would never have come to this neighborhood even though my family was here. This was something they would do belittle themselves, but I would never mix with the likes of these people. I went on in trying not to let how I really felt show on my face and took a seat next to my husband, then whatever this was got started Ms. Mattie got up and said a prayer, then Shun's sisters got up to talk about the occasion. Ms. Mattie sat down with tears in her eyes, thanking God for a day she thought would never happen and that she would never see, her daughter being drug free and the completion of any program. She was so happy and they all had gifts for the twins.

They knew that Beth did not want a shower because the babies would be well taken care of and she didn't want to put them through any unnecessary expense, but there was plenty of stuff for them there and Mi'lan had plenty of gifts too. Ms. Mattie called Mi'lan up front to speak. Elizabeth nearly flipped out of her seat, she thought she was going to make a grand entrance, so who she thought was her sister was actually her.

"I must admit she looks good, even though she beat me out of my money I can't say anything."
When Mi'Ian saw her come in she left out for a minute but was back before her mother called her up if they could do the shower portion first and then she would come back and speak towards the end. They played shower games, they opened gifts, then they ate. Beth's father and Jr. said they couldn't recall having that much fun, they thought everything was great. Shun and Beth thanked everyone and to make sure their names were on their gift because they would certainly be receiving a birth announcement. Elizabeth was sitting there wishing everything would hurry up and end.

CHAPTER 30

No sooner than she had thought that, Mi'lan walked back up to the front. She too wanted to thank everyone for their support and their prayers during her stint in rehab. Lizabeth thought, *Oh, that's where she was and why she didn't contact me. She knew before she took my money she was going there, she probably had a last fling in the crack house before she left with my money.*

"Just to tell you a little bit about why I chose to go, some of you already know my story but for those of you who may not know, I have been addicted to crack most of my children's entire life. I got involved with the wrong crowd and also looking for love in all the wrong places. I've done some things that I am not proud of and I'm ashamed for myself. I left my kids on my mother, dropped baby after baby on her. I know it wasn't right but I only cared about myself and what I wanted to do. I've begged, stole, and borrowed and lied and even sold my body for some twos and few, I had no intentions of paying anybody back."

Elizabeth said, "Hymp."

"Now when I found out my son was expecting a baby with Beth, not only a baby but twins, my first grands, I thought I am going to turn my life around and be the best grandmother I can be. It hasn't been easy but I am going to do this, in fact I was tested in a mighty way just a few days before I was to check myself into rehab and I knew if I could pass that test I was going to be a recovering addict the rest of my life. All I could do was thank God for keeping me in the right frame of mind."

Elizabeth thought, *Where is this going?* In her mind she was saying, *Please, please don't mention me, surely she's not.*

Just as she thought that Mi'lan walked over to her and said, "Here's your $10,000 dollars, just like you gave it to me. On the one hand you nearly allowed me to be at the point of no return or death, but on the other hand you helped to free me from bondage, so by the grace of God I am standing here."

She sunk way down in her seat.

"For those of you, especially Shun and Beth, Beth, your mother had someone find me, I met with her, she gave me $10,000 dollars to talk Shun into leaving you and breaking the two of you up. That way she could prove that he is no good and wasn't going to be there for you, that way she could convince her to abort the one baby we thought she was having. We now know that it is twins, before it was too late I took the money with devious thoughts."

Mi'lan was interrupted by Beth's father saying, "Elizabeth, how could you?"

She wanted to deny everything until Mi'lan threw a picture of them on the table.

Jr. said, "You should be ashamed of yourself."

Judge Tirans said, "Let's go, you don't have to say anything," but Shun said, "Please let me say something before you leave. Does my upbringing, the clothes I wear, or the hand I've been dealt sentence me to life? It is possible to rise above, it doesn't mean I have to be a statistic. I am going to succeed and let me leave this with you: I am not ashamed of where I live or my circumstances. They have only matured me and made me thirst for the best. I am being prepared and been given the incentive to really work toward my goals. I am going to know to teach my children morals and values, love, and most importantly not to think of themselves more than they ought to thank you."
They were all so hurt and Beth's family was so embarrassed, just to think she faked a change of heart.
Beth's father asked if he could speak. He went up front, talked about how much he had enjoyed himself, and he apologized profusely for this predicament. He asked that they please, please forgive her and that nothing like that would ever happen again. Then they left.
She looked like a sick puppy. "How will I ever be able to make up for this? I may lose my family behind this. I should have left well enough alone. I'd rather crawl into a hole and stay there rather than face my husband and family once we were home."

CHAPTER 31

Once they made it to the car, it was silence all the way home. She wished he would say something, rant or rave, but nothing. She knew she had really messed up this time because normally he would have started as soon as they were outside. When they made it home she went straight into his office so that they could get it over with.

He said, "Not tonight, I am going to shower and turn in for the night. I have to do some thinking about this one. Goodnight."

No matter what I always came out on top, but I was not so sure he was not going to leave me, was I going to lose my family? It seemed that with this whole pregnancy thing and the lowlife family my daughter had gotten herself involved in had been the most difficult task to master what was really going on. What could I say or do to keep my husband and my family together? It would be so embarrassing for my friends to not only find out that Beth was pregnant by some boy from the projects and my husband had left me. I must also get my thoughts together and I knew she was not going to want any-

thing to do with me for a while if not forever. I was only trying to keep her from ruining her life and reputation. Think, think, Elizabeth, I have to be ready for this one in the morning.

CHAPTER 32

I went on upstairs to get ready for bed. I walked into the bedroom and as I did I said, "Walter?" ready to apologize and say something. He wasn't there. The bed hadn't been disturbed. Oh my goodness, he didn't even want to be in the same room with me. He was in one of the guest rooms. I had to convince him that I wouldn't interfere anymore even though I still wanted to fight this, even though I knew she was way too far along for an abortion. It was a shame that I didn't know how many months she was. I had a pretty good guess but nevertheless nothing specific. To be honest, I really hadn't had any interest in knowing, I just wanted it to be over with. I had to accept things now, I had to plead for another chance. I had to learn to stop trying to have things go my way. Where did I go wrong? I gave my children everything you could imagine. I thought that was enough for them to make the right choices. They had never, ever wanted for anything. We lived in one of the most expensive homes in our gated community. They had the best of everything, and then Beth went and got hooked up with a family that had nothing, no home, no car, absent father, and a crackhead for a mother, why? Why? I didn't deserve this. I just laid there in the dark struggling to fall asleep. I just kept thinking in the morning all hell was going to break loose.

CHAPTER 33

When I awakened to get ready to go to the hospital, I had a serious surgery this morning so I sat in the sunroom with a cup of coffee, trying to collect my thoughts so I could focus for what lies ahead this morning. I always took the time to meditate before I got dressed to leave so I couldn't really put a lot of thought into last night. I wouldn't be able to live with myself if I made a mistake, although I was considered one of the best in my field. I was known around the world a woman that was so successful had to be worried about her young daughter becoming a mother. It just wasn't fair, my son was not causing me any heartaches and pains just enjoying his life and his toys. I hoped he didn't follow in his sister's footsteps even though he was the oldest. Oh well, I must get to the hospital. I could see Walter had left for the day, he left earlier than usual. I guess he didn't want to see my face, he must really be upset. I'd rather we get this over with. I didn't do silence very well. I was a little worried and afraid, no one was talking to me except the staff. I was sure they didn't always want to since they were paid. They had no other choice and I paid them good.

CHAPTER 34

Beth was lying awake thinking about last night. She had been awake for about forty-five minutes to an hour, knowing that if she didn't believe in the power of prayer she wouldn't have gotten any rest, so after praying she slept like a baby. Just when she thought her mother was done with all of her tricks, she pulled the biggest one yet. Her father asked her to please not be upset and to let him handle this for the last time. He let her know how much he enjoyed himself and that Shun had a wonderful family and that he knew they were proud of the progress his mother had made. He asked if it was okay if he attended church with them on Sunday. She was so happy, he said he could see a difference in her since she had been attending church, how calm she was about things now that Jr. was going. He said he would be every time he was home from school, she said she would love for him to come. I told him about dinner and asked if he wanted to take everyone out because of where they lived. He told me to stick to the usual plan, that way he could learn more about the family.

Her cell phone rang, it was Shun checking on her to see if she got any rest and if she was okay. After last night she told him she was fine. She came in and prayed about it and she wasn't going to dwell on it.

"I hope that you are okay as well," and she prayed he wasn't too embarrassed. He stated again he was not going to be made to feel bad about his life and his upbringing. She was happy he was okay.

"If you think she can run me off and make me abandon you think again, I'm sticking and I'm staying," said Shun.

"Thanks, Shun, I love you too. I'm hanging up now, talk to you later."

CHAPTER 35

Well, it was Sunday and Walter hadn't said anything to Elizabeth about the incident and she had been too afraid to bring it up. He had been cordial to her but nothing more, he was still sleeping in one of the guest rooms and the only reason he hadn't moved out was because Beth didn't seem too devastated, so he was glad to be going to church with them to see and hear what was keeping her going during all that was going on in her life. She hadn't once complained about her mother's actions. As a matter of fact, she hadn't brought it up. So it was time for them to leave. They still took multiple cars so that they could give everyone a ride. Beth called Shun when they reached the complex so everyone could start to come outside. They got in the cars, they always arrived early so they could be seated together. They took up two rows but that was okay.

Church began, then Ms. Mattie had a solo, then she surprised them by asking Shun to join her. So he went up and they sang together. The song's title was "My Story." Beth was in tears.

She had no idea that he could sing, then the sermon started. "Who do you choose to serve?"

Walter sat there listening. He asked God what would he have him to do concerning his wife's actions. He first asked him to forgive him for his sins and he invited him into his life, something that he had never, ever thought to do. He felt an instant calm come overtake him. He felt that he didn't have a care in the world right then.

"Now I understand how Beth can be so at peace. Wow, this is pretty good, it looks as if just stepping in God's house lifts the heaviness off you. I think this is where I need to be on Sundays instead of on the golf course."

The sermon was just what he needed. He almost stood the whole time thanking God that he allowed him to still be alive and apologizing for never thanking him for blessing them with all that they had and to witness the first time in his adult life that he came to church on his own without being invited, and he only accepted a few invitations, then he had tears streaming down his face. He was thinking, *I haven't been living, only existing.*

The pastor was a middle-aged man that was truly anointed, so when the sermon was over and the doors of the church were opened he leaned over to Beth and whispered that he had wasted enough time, he was joining.

He, Beth, Jr., and Symie stood. They all walked down and the pastor called for Shun, he whispered in his ear the song he loved to hear him sing and asked if he would do it, Beth could not believe he could sing so well, he never mentioned it. When they were taken in the back they asked for family prayer and they specifically asked for prayer for Elizabeth. Mi'lan even came in the back. Once they were done they all left to go and have dinner. Ms. Mattie and Mi'lan had prepared ribs, chicken, collard greens, mac/cheese, okra, yams, cornbread, tea, and for dessert butter pound cake. The dinner was fabulous. They had good conversation and laughter. The younger ones asked to be excused when they were done eating, they carried their dishes to the kitchen. They were so very well mannered and polite and Walter was in shock as to how clean and neat their apartment was, nothing was out of place. He offered to pay her for all of that cooking but she refused, he told her that he wouldn't feel so bad for eating so much if she accepted the money and to purchase the food for the next two Sundays, one for him, one for Jr.'s day, then it would be back to her turn. He wouldn't leave until she agreed that they would alternate.

CHAPTER 36

Walter laid three one-hundred-dollar bills on the table. Ms. Mattie went to catch him to tell him that was too much money. He put his hands to his lips to silence her. She just said, "Thank you," and they drove off. He felt that he was on cloud nine. He couldn't express how much the day had meant to him; it was as if it were the best day of his life. He had been thinking about moving out after that stunt Elizabeth pulled, but the strangest thing happened in church. Something said, "Forgive her."

"I wonder where that came from. If I decide to stay I really have to put my foot down about her selfish and conniving ways. She has to know it will no longer be tolerated and if she doesn't think she can change her ways, it will be best if he left now. If she chooses for us to stay married she has to get her act together."

He was still in awe at the closeness of Shun's family. "I mean, it doesn't matter where you live so that's not what I'm saying, but if you listen to my wife they can't do anything right. Their grandmother has done a very good job in raising those kids, she could be paid by teaching others how to raise and train their children, God bless her. Now I have to think about my life and the changes that are going to take place. We will start new members on Wednesday night and Beth had asked me the one-hundred-million-dollar question: Wonder if Mom will ever join? I am going to have a long talk with her tonight. I thanked her for letting me tag along and she said thank you for asking."

CHAPTER 37

Elizabeth was home from her rounds. She was wondering where everyone was. Rosalita told her they all went to church.

"Are you sure they went to church, Walter?"

"Yes, my, my, my—"

Just then the door opened, everyone walked in. Walter spoke, he looked so calm, his whole demeanor seemed different. He asked me to meet him in the sunroom in forty-five minutes. *Forty five minutes? Why now and what is he about to do?* is what she thought as she began to thumb through a magazine to pass the time. He needed to talk to her. She was wondering, what was he about to say or do, why forty-five minutes, why not now? She decided to go on in and thumb through a magazine, maybe if he passed by he would come on in but he didn't come out of that bedroom until exactly that time he walked in, and I took a deep breath.

Here goes.

"Let me start by saying I was prepared to move out."

She gasped. "Hold on," Walter said. "Up until this morning, I felt your actions were unwarranted against Beth and Shun, and just about unforgivable the way you refuse to stand by our own daughter. This last one was what put the icing on the cake, but when I noticed how calm Beth was and the fact that she never falls apart, she informed me that attending church and her relationship with God are the only thing that has kept her sane.

"Really?" exclaimed Elizabeth "Is it that huge church on the corner and how could you go without me?"

"Well, first of all we went to Shun's family's church and we joined there. Secondly I am so glad that I did, it is giving us, you and me, another chance. God has allowed me to have forgiveness in my heart for what I feel like is some strange reason I felt like I didn't need to wait, I felt that I did what I needed to do for my sanity."

"You mean you joined a church in the hood?"

"If that's what you want to refer to it as." She said to herself, *If he thinks I would even consider going to the hood, he can think again.*

CHAPTER 38

"I can assure you that there are going to be some changes made around here. We have been truly blessed; we never even considered going to church around here or serving the Lord, much less showing gratitude for the life he allows us to live, and it's long overdue. You don't want to stand by the kids but look at what they are doing and how they are trying to do the right thing after making a huge mistake in their lives."

"Walter, you only went to church one time and now you think that's all it takes? What happened to you, what did they do to you, is that church some kind of cult or do they practice witchcraft?"

"No, Elizabeth, none of the above, they did nothing to me, just the atmosphere, the peace, the sermon, and the prayer for us.

"It just made me feel like I needed to change and draw closer to the Lord, and the fact that he guided me on what to do in my marriage, you can look in my closet and see that I had been packing to move out, but I asked God what will he have me do, and that was to forgive you."

The only reason I didn't leave was because I didn't want Beth to be upset, and on top of that left here with you. That's a shame that I was afraid to leave your own daughter here with you but believe it or not, she would have been fine because she wouldn't have dealt with you or your games. The relationship she is developing with the Lord is fantastic so I need you to hear me and hear me good. She is having her babies and we are going to support her, all of your games are stopping now. If for some reason you cannot get it together and I find out you have tried something else, you will be the one moving out, did I make myself clear?"

"Yes."

"Are there any questions?"

"No."

"I understand your job and we can never tell when you will be off, but if at all possible, we need to attend church as a family. If you don't want to do that you can attend a church of your choice but I'm staying where I am."

Hymp, before I attend that church I will be planning as many surgeries on Sundays as I possibly can, I may even make that my main day except for emergencies, this was what she was thinking to herself. *What makes him think he can control me? I have no plans of changing, did not have plans of being a grandparent at this young age. I'm sorry, I just can't get excited, what are my friends saying behind my back? I'm sure they know just because I never bring it up, they keep silent, what did I do to deserve this? I've worked hard and long to get to the top. God didn't send me to school or even pay for my schooling. I did it all with my smarts and my folks' money. I made it to the top without his help and I don't need him now, even my best friend in all the world doesn't know about all of my business and I'm certainly not telling her about Beth. I'm glad she lives in another state.*

"Elizabeth, you seem to be in another world. I was talking to you, are we clear on everything? Do you have any questions? No, one last thing, has it ever occurred to you that we need to accept some of the fault if not all of it that this happened to Beth?"

"How can you say that or even think that?"

"Just think about it for a minute, when do we spend time with them, when was the last time we had a family vacation, when have we sat down with them to try and find out what was going on in their lives or even their days we didn't even let them pick out their cars, we bought them what we wanted them to have, so we can accept a lot of the blame for allowing them free reign. I've had a lot of time to think being in the guest room. I suggest you take some time to look over your life and what kind of mother you have been to your children. Jr. is in school and about to be an adult, the least we can do is try to help out as much as we can with our grandchildren."

The thought of that word sickened her. *I'm just too young for this. I will not babysit or have anything to do with them, but I will try and be civilized, it's going to be hard but I will try. I don't know how this is going to turn out, at least I have all of my money back and that crackhead didn't smoke it up. I just think if she had of lived up to her side of the bargain, we wouldn't be having this discussion and things would be back normal; we would be going on with life but instead dealing with this mess with Beth has almost broken up my family. I'll never forgive her for this, everybody's attention is focused on her, she has caused my husband to turn on me and I'm not running things like I always have. Who does she think she is? I can answer that myself: a fifteen-year-old mother to be dummy.*

CHAPTER 39

Elizabeth decided a few mornings to leave earlier than usual. She could always fake an emergency so early morning hours were a good excuse, so lately she had been away more than usual, which was fine with Beth. It didn't matter to her if she was there or not, she continued to pray for her mother and she prayed to keep her peace about her. At her last appointment the doctor said the babies were fine, she was doing great. Even though she was getting real big he didn't see her having an early delivery, but that you never know with multiple births. She and Shun were so happy, he had found another job and he was working after school and still at McDonald's on the weekend but he was off today. He asked for as many hours as he could get, he was only going to work at McDonald's until the babies were born to save as much as he could. They were going shopping to pick up some things for the babies. He was so excited about being able to pay for everything even though Beth didn't want him to and asked if they could each pay half, but he wasn't having it, he already said he was going to be the best father he could be to his children and to her.

After they finished and had dinner together they went to their favorite spot. They walked and discussed some more things. Beth told him again how much she appreciated him for keeping his word.

She said, "I don't mean to offend you, it's just that I am so grateful."

He didn't say anything but just thanked her because after all he had seen a lot of his friends run out on the girls and leave them alone to fend for themselves with a baby, so he truly understood where she was coming from. They decided to go on in because this would be Jr.'s last Sunday for a while. It was time for him to leave for school. He asked if we would mail him the DVD from every Sunday. We told him we would, he also said he was going to find him a church where he could visit until he was home.

He even committed to staying focused and on track. He was going to work hard and read his Bible. He was so happy that he started attending church. He said he didn't know the Lord before now and that he wasn't turning his back on him now that he knew a little about him. It had only opened his eyes to learning more about him. He really wished his parents had taken them when they were younger but it is what it is. He was not blaming anyone but from this day forward he would be taking matters into his own hands.

CHAPTER 40

Church was awesome as usual. They had a special prayer for all students and they even had a committee set up so all of them that needed prayer and encouragement or found themselves not able to stay on track could contact them either by phone, email, or text. It was something they were trying on a trial basis and the first-time college students were all excited about it. They felt a sense of comfort knowing that they had this kind of service at their disposal. Jr. fellowshipped with the pastor and his family, then we all left for dinner. They had outdone themselves again. Ms. Mattie looked like she tried to spend every dime of that money as much food as she had prepared, every drop of it was delicious. She had even made a big butter roll, something that we had never heard of, and it was off the chain. She cooked two cakes, we were all so full we could hardly walk to the cars. Dad slipped three hundred more dollars in Ms. Mattie's apron with a note to give half to Mi'lan and said he was not trying to pay them, it was just a tip. He was going to tell Beth to let them know he was taking everyone out next Sunday so she wouldn't purchase or prepare food.

Once they made it home Elizabeth was sitting in the sunroom. She came out to greet them, asked how everyone was, and apologized for not being home much but that she had been so busy with all of her cases. She thought to herself she had to start somewhere but it certainly wasn't going to be that church. She wanted no parts of it, that was their thing. Walter gave her a hug and a kiss on her cheek, said he was good, and so did the others. She didn't ask anything and they didn't offer anything, she wanted to know what they wanted to do for dinner, if they wanted to eat at home or go out to dinner. They all said they had a super dinner and that Ms. Mattie and Mi'lan had prepared it. She just said okay, so everyone left to chill for a while, then she asked Walter if he would like to go to the movies. He said he wanted to lie down and take a nap. He interrupted her thoughts, "I went showered and changed, I said I couldn't lay down if I wanted to but since I see you are trying how much time do you need before we can leave?"

CHAPTER 41

She made it back to the sunroom and she was just like she was before they came home alone.

"Is this how you feel when you give up your control? Do you feel alone and lost if you are not running things? We'll see. I'll lay low for a minute, I haven't really been paying much attention to Beth but she is really getting huge. I know they must be very busy in there since it's two. I remember how it felt when Jr. kicked for the first time, it was the best feeling. Wait a minute, girlfriend, don't even go there, why do you even care what it feels like? You know you have no interest in any of that. I shouldn't have let any of that foolishness even enter my mind. I'll just turn on the computer and play some poker and wait and see what happens. When Walter wakes up I'm sure he's not going anywhere with me."

He interrupted her thoughts. "I went and showered and changed, I said I couldn't lie down if I wanted to after, it seems like you are trying, how much time do you need before we can leave?"

She was in shock. "10 minutes maybe."

"What do you have in mind to see?"

"Uh, I haven't checked to see what's playing."

"That's okay, we'll check and then if it's too early we'll just grab some tea or coffee, are you hungry?"

"We can get you something and I'll just drink something," she said she'd be right back. "Well, just knock me off my feet."

Chapter 42

Beth didn't even come back downstairs, she was so full it seemed like she slept forever, then Shun called her on his break. They talked for a minute she told him she was still stuffed and could hardly stay awake she just needed to soak, she was growing by leaps and bounds. Dr. Rancifer told her the babies are going to be a nice size, then Shun asked if she was okay? "She said yes, just a little tired." They said a quick prayer and then she went to soak for a while. She was about to step in, there was a knock on the door. It was Symie. Her dad asked her to come and check on her on their way out the door, she let her know she was about to soak in the tub. She told her to call on the intercom if she needed her, gave her a hug, and they each said "I love you." She stayed in there about an hour, then she lotioned her body and sat in her recliner and watched television for a while. She felt so at peace before she closed her eyes for the night. She read over her notes from church and prayed some then fell asleep.

When she woke up the next morning, she realized she had

fallen asleep in the chair. She thought that was funny, said it slept almost as good as her bed. KeKe called as soon as she stood up to ask how she was and said she was coming home with her to spend the night.

"Good, maybe I won't sleep so much, I'll ask Rosie to cook our favorite."

"Sounds good to me."

"I need to get dressed, see you later."

When Beth came down everyone was gone. Jr. was still asleep, Dad was going with him later on to make sure he was settled in. They were going to fly out on a private plane, that way Dad could come back later on or early morning. He was having afternoon court, for this reason he was all excited but at the same time we knew we were going to be missing each other. We've never been apart for a long time and we have been praying together, we said we were going to be fine. I really could not afford to be upset; I was trying to stay as stress free as possible so I thought it best that I am not around when he left. They decided to leave after I was gone, I didn't even want to know the time they were leaving.

CHAPTER 43

I was so glad that KeKe was spending the night. We chatted, had dinner, played the Xbox connect even though I played laying back in the recliner. We did karaoke, we watched videos, laughed, caught up on things, and I told her she could have the bed, that I wanted to sleep in the recliner. We kept laughing and talking even though we knew we had to get up early. Shun had already made his nightly call, he had been so busy working. I really only got to see him at school, some Saturdays but every Sunday. When KeKe heard us praying she asked about church and asked if she could join us sometime. I told her, "Sure, whenever you are ready." We had a really good time. She said she understood, that I had a lot going on and that I seemed so happy and peaceful. She said if that were her she'd be all over the place with fear and not knowing what to do I probably would have been too if it were not for Shun and his family and my dad, but most importantly learning how to trust and depend on God and my favorite prayer, if you promise to live according to God's will he will lead, guide, and direct you. Wow, that's deep, it's deeper than you can ever imagine. I have Shun to thank for introducing me to the power of prayer.

"Will you please get with me real soon so you can go over the steps I need to take to get me to where you are?"

"Well, I'm still in the beginning stages. Ms. Mattie says things are not going to happen overnight and that you must stay rooted and grounded, it doesn't mean that you will be perfect and it doesn't mean you won't make mistakes. Read your Bible and pray."

"Sounds very interesting."

"Well, I could go on and on, we'd better get out of here, you know that I love you."

"I love you more."

CHAPTER 44

It was time for Beth to be making weekly visits, with school being the biggest of her activities, she mostly stayed home in the evenings. If she wanted to go somewhere Jeffrey drove her, when she wanted to give Symie a break Jeffrey drove her to school every day. She was always tired, she had grown by leaps and bounds. This was her last week in school, she would have a homebound teacher for a little while now, she didn't feel bad but she felt like she was hauling two sand bags. Her dad would always stop her and put his hands on her stomach and teasingly ask "how are Clarence and Clara doing?", and she would laugh and say "Daddy I would never name my babies old-fashioned names like those." Her mother was sitting there that day just looking but would never get involved in their conversation. The most she would ask was "How are you and the babies?" She never asked how many months she was or if she needed anything or the babies needed anything or if she had a bag packed or what she needed in the bag. She just couldn't bring herself to show any interest. Beth thought to herself, *That's fine with me, this way I can stay calm, keep my peace, and not have to wonder if she is up to anything. I really need my mother at this time, I've needed her the whole time but she is too selfish to give of herself, but I can't afford to risk my life and the life of my unborn twins trying to see where her head is and wondering if she loves me. I mean, it's not like we had an unbreakable bond anyway, she cares more for her job than me. I think I just keep asking God to keep me focused on the situation at hand and not let the thoughts of my mother's actions consume me, this way I am able to keep it moving. I care about how she feels, I even care about what she thinks of me, but on the other hand look at how she treats me.*

CHAPTER 45

Elizabeth was thinking to herself, *Why haven't I been able to embrace this thing? It is almost over with, why can't I let my guard down? I'm not involved nor do I want to be, how can I this late in the game, pretend I care? I shouldn't have to be threatened with divorce just because of her stupidity, why does my marriage have to suffer because my one and only daughter wanted to play adult games?*

Even though I know he has forgiven me, I know we should have taken the time to discuss the birds and the bees but since our lives are so busy that's why we have household help that's available to them and we pay them well, that should stand for something. Some people are not there for their children and can't afford to hire help so she could have shown some kind of appreciation for the life she lives and not gotten herself pregnant. I still would like to know what was she thinking and then she was co-mingling with the likes of those people fellowshipping, having dinner out in public, what is my family being reduced to? I know some of my friends and colleagues have seen them out together, maybe the think they are my housekeeper's family but then I'm sure they display some kind of affection and they also see Beth's bulge. Oh well, maybe I'll just invite them out to the country club for brunch and bridge and tell them what they probably already know, just haven't heard it from me, but because I've been silent they have to, my thoughts are running wild, what is she going to have them call me, Dr. Liz? Mrs. Tirans? Just the thought of being called Grandmother or Big Mama or Memaw at this age, but these are my grandchildren. I have got to practice changing my heart. I could never let her know my thoughts, what else will they call me other than Grandmother? I have had to work hard not to let this interfere with my work. I have to be cool, calm, and collected when I'm operating on my patients. I can't afford to let my home life spill over into my work life. I have too many sick people whose lives depend on my hands. I've always been able to keep a level head, I've always been able to be stress free and have the mindset and ability to save many lives, the lives I've saved far outweigh the ones lost, most of the time they were already gone before I touched them, looks as though I may need to save me from me. I should be able to handle this situation better than I'm handling it. I guess I made my own plans for everybody else's life and didn't think about them making their own plans. Will I ever be able to get over this and adjust? Right now it doesn't seem like it, maybe later.

CHAPTER 46

Well, as luck would have it, or should I say the lack of luck, the three of us wound up at breakfast at the same time. It was awkward for me trying to blend in with Walter and Beth chatting so easily. We spoke, Beth even had a smile on her face. I asked what was going on, they both said, "Same ole, same ole." Beth looked huge. I thought dang, how could a child so young be so big? I shouldn't have been surprised with twins, I didn't know of anybody in my family with twins. I knew you really had to get big to have them.

Beth said, "Mom, how are you feeling this morning?"

I said, "Uh, good, I'm good, and yourself?"

"I'm good too, just a little tired. I can't get comfortable anymore."

"Then I guess that is a problem."

Walter asked if I was on call for the day only for something the other on-call doctor can't handle. I was glad he asked the question when he did because I didn't know how to make conversation, then Beth said she had to get ready to leave for her appointment. Walter stood and hugged her since she had to pass by him, I asked if I could have one, she did so but had an unsure look on her face. I could tell she wondered if I was serious, she was still my child and I trusted this would all work out in the end.

CHAPTER 47

Well, Beth and the babies were still doing good, she was very uncomfortable but good. One baby was really active and all over the place, it seemed well.

"We are about to get to the finish line, are you excited?"

"Sure I am, will my stomach go back in place after being stretched so wide?"

"Sure, but you may have to do a little exercising but you should be fine. Women's bodies are made for this, then they pop back into place, any questions?"

"No."

"Well, call, don't hesitate to call if you have any problems or questions, see you next week, thank you."

Beth and Symie left.

"Is there anything you want to do?"

"Well, it's early, why don't we call Ms. Mattie and see what they're up to and visit for a while?"

"That sounds good but first I'll call Shun and give him an update."

They talked for about ten minutes, then prayed and hung up.
She told him her plans to call his grandmother. He said,
"Good, she will be glad to hear from you." He said he might
make it home before she left if all went as planned. When she
called Ms. Mattie was glad to hear from them. She invited them
on over, said she would have lunch ready. They asked if they
could bring lunch with them. She said no, she was only preparing a light lunch but they could bring sodas and chips. They
were more than happy to, of course, they bought a little more
than she asked. Once there they sat down and talked to Mi'lan
and the kids for about thirty minutes before lunch was served.
Mi'lan was still holding on, said she was making sure that she
made all of her meetings and the kids looked so happy, they
were finally calming down. They were always thinking that she
was going to fall off the wagon again. Every time she saw the
kids they wanted to touch her stomach to feel the babies kicking. They thought that was so funny and I would say something
to them as the babies kicked. They went in, had lunch, sat there
for an hour just sitting and talking. As they all finally calmed
down, they thought to themselves she might fall off the wagon
again. Whenever the kids saw Beth, they wanted to touch her
stomach, the feeling of the baby kicking was absolutely amusing
to them; it tickled her. They went in had lunch for about an
hour just sitting and talking. All the kids had been excused,
Beth then asked if they wouldn't mind moving back so she
could get comfortable on the sofa.

"Sorry we sat here so long."

"That's okay" said Milan, "I am enjoying the chat, oh and by
the way I ran into Shun's father the other day, he didn't even
recognize me and I wasn't sure if I should make him aware of

who I was." "I'm going to follow God's direction on this decision I make just in case we encounter each other once again." "I
don't know if he still lives here or if he is just visiting from out
of town but what I do know is I don't want any of this mentioned to Shun right now." "Ok, I understand." said Beth.

"Hey!" Ms.Ma ttie said, "Why don't we look at pictures of
Shun growing up?" Beth replied, "You know what? I would love
that." Milan thought to herself, *I haven't seen these pictures in
years and I'm not even sure if I would remember them."* They spent
the next hour looking at pictures laughing and discussing the
many stories that came with them. We were about to leave
when Shun showed up and we ended up sitting and talking for
about another hour. Then the evening ended with a prayer and
we finally left.

At first Beth didn't know if she would feel up to attending
church tomorrow, if at all possible she would because she knew
that real soon she would be missing a few. Dad and Symie
started new members orientation on Wednesday night, but I
decided to wait because I wouldn't want to start and not be able
to finish the entire session at one time. After arriving home
Beth chatted with her dad for a minute before going up to her
room to rest. She was so exhausted couldn't even make it to the
shower and ended up napping before she could get in. Beth always made it a point to leave the door unlocked just in case she
needed assistance.

CHAPTER 48

She made it to church after all and was blessed by it. Shun asked the pastor for a special prayer for Beth and the twins because he was feeling that it wasn't going to be long before Beth would be out for a minute, so he prayed for them. They left and went to one of Ms. Mattie's favorite soul food restaurants even though she didn't get to go there very often it was just as good as ever and her good friend Lowe still ran one of the top restaurants in the city. She came out and was introduced to everyone. Lowe still ran a top-of-the-line place. She came out and was introduced to them. They got ready to leave, then Walter asked if they wanted to do something different. He asked who wanted to go to the movies. The kids all shouted "We do!" but the adults were all too tired. Of course, Beth was worn out, so Shun and Walter took all of the kids to the movies. They were so excited. Symie and Beth headed home so she could prop her feet up and get some rest. This was really the beginning of a true family affair. They really enjoyed the blended family. The only one not excited was Elizabeth. Beth thought to herself, *What is it going to take? It's nearly time for me to deliver and she hasn't been here for me, never asks how I am or the babies, hasn't bought one thing for us. I just keep praying that things will change for them if not for me because I'm nearing the end of the line for me. I won't be carrying them too much longer but she is a hard nut to crack, even though I'm at peace I'm not going to say this does not bother me. This is my mother and I love her regardless. Sometimes I need to know, hear, and feel that she loves me too. I would love for her to put her arms around me and tell me that she loves me in spite of my mistakes and we both feel the babies kicking together; instead I've gone through this whole pregnancy without any support from her. Dear God, how long? Will she ever change? Does she even pray or know how? Does she believe in you? I just don't know what to think or do. I'm going to continue to pray for her and let her be. I sometimes see how nervous she seems to be when I'm around, that really hurts. I know that I messed up. I not only disappointed my parents, I disappointed myself. I let myself down. I'm not proud of my actions, if I could have made all of this go away I would have as soon as it happened. I'm now learning that things happen for a reason but I can't waddle in it, I must keep it moving. Last but not least, there are consequences for your actions. I had big plans for myself and my life, never in my wildest dreams would I have thought I would be pregnant at fifteen years old and not with one child but two, but I am going to be the best mother I can be. I'm going to make the best of this. I'm not taking a break no more than allowed for childbirth. I'm going to jump right back in, complete all of my schooling. Thank God I have a great support system. Even if I didn't get pregnant Shun would have still been my flavor, and the fact that he knows a lot about the Lord is the icing on the cake not to mention he's so mature for his age. Thank you, Lord, and I know you have forgiven us, why can't my mom?*

CHAPTER 49

Well, now I had been out of school for a minute, I enjoyed relaxing and spending lots of time with Symie. After I was done with the schoolwork, we looked through all of the things I had for the babies and for myself. We packed the bag for the hospital, and of course I stopped driving a while ago. She also told me it was best that every appointment that I take my packed bags along just in case, it may seem like a lot of trouble but you never know. Symie took good care of me, I already let her know that I expected her there with us and also discussed with Shun her being their godmother, along with KeKe. I told her she is the Jr. godmother, she agreed but didn't want any problems from my mother. I told Keke that my mother has no interest in me or the babies, I don't feel she even ever cared really. "I mean no harm when I say that but it should make you feel really bad" said Symie. Beth simply replied with "Indeed it does." I asked him to bless her and I also asked him to forgive her for treating me this way, and if I asked him then I had to forgive her also. I was her child and she should love me unconditionally, so since I made a huge mistake or every time I make a mistake was this what I could expect? Would she disown me? I really didn't know what to think. I knew not to expect her in the delivery room holding my hand since I knew I couldn't depend on her. I'm not okay but I am okay if that makes sense. I have kept my hand in Gods hand and he has been leading and guiding me all along, so in a little while my life is going to change and take on a new meaning. I would be a mother, a parent, and with all of my being I was going to be good and understanding if and when my children made mistakes. I mean I was sure they were going to make plenty. I would see them through with much love and discipline. I didn't want them to keep making the same ones. I would teach them to learn from them, try not to make them over and over and move on. I was going to raise them with respect and let them know I didn't expect them to be perfect. They would spend lots of time with Shun's family so they would understand what true love was all about, and because they would be living a different lifestyle than my family didn't make ours any better than theirs. We were all God's children no matter what.

CHAPTER 50

Shun called to check on us, wanting to know how all of his babies were. I said, "We are all good, even though I feel like a large kangaroo with my pouch full, and I am wondering what my visit will be like on Saturday. My stomach is so tight and it doesn't seem like it is as high as it has been. I must confess, I am a tad bit nervous, wondering what the unknown is going to be like, how do you feel about us becoming parents real soon?"

"Well, I don't know what to expect, but I'm up for the challenge, this is our doing. We're in this together and we're going to be fine."

"I'm glad we have been praying the whole time, it really relieves the stress of it all."

"Yes, it does, Beth. I have one question to ask, I'm not trying to upset you, but what's going to happen when you go home from the hospital? "You know my family is not welcomed in your home, I've never been there and that is a big concern of mine. I want to be there for you and my babies. I know that you are going to be down for a couple of weeks and I don't want to be away from you, all I need is to be able to do my part. I know that you all have staff but you all are a part of me. I thought about this a lot but I didn't mention it, I guess I was trying to see if she was going to come around but nothing has changed."

"Thank you, because I have been thinking about it quite a bit. We have the nursery all together, we have a sitting area with two rockers and it has a queen-sized sofa bed, so you will be able to sleep over and help out, but I will have to speak to my dad first. They certainly don't have to worry about us sneaking around because I will be trying to recuperate. We have a far more important task at hand, we've got to get finished with school, then head off to college. We can't allow this to happen again until we are older and much more mature and most importantly married."

"Married?"

"Yes, is that something that you would even consider between the two of us?"

us?"

"Of course, why wouldn't I?" said Beth. "I love you, I enjoy you, and you accepted me for who I am. You did not judge me in spite of your teachings, and I don't want any other man raising my children. I am going to show your mother a thing or two, and on that note I feel that I can spend the rest of my life with you."

"Oh, that's so sweet of you to say. I have no doubt that I can spend eternity with you, but let's just grow up and mature a little more. I'm sure after twins we're going to be a little more something."

They both laughed.

"Okay, well, you have that talk with your dad and let me know how it turns out, good or bad. "Be honest with me Beth, okay? Now let's say our daily prayer then continue relaxing okay Big Momma??"

"Okay, that cracks me up when you call me that, but there's no denying it."

They finished and said goodbye.

CHAPTER 51

Beth was normally taking a nap or relaxing when her dad came home, but today she made a point to tell Symie to let her dad know she wanted to speak to him when he came in. "Tell him to wake me up if I am asleep."
She decided to spend some time double checking her bags to make sure she had everything she thought she would need.
She already went over everything with Symie just passing time. She took a moment and said a quick prayer and she was okay, just going over the discussion about her mother's actions was causing her to think a little more and she definitely didn't need any undue stress. It was something going on in the way she was feeling that was concerning her. The babies were moving about as usual, didn't know if both were moving a lot or just one, but the doctor said they were both fine. Her mind kept drifting off, then there was a knock on her door. It was Symie letting her know her dad was home. He wanted to know if she wanted to come down or if he should come up.
She asked if her mom was home yet.

She said, "No, and you can never tell when she will show up."
"Yeah, you are right about that, just tell him he can come up
when he has time, thank you."
"I'll go right down and tell him."
About fifteen minutes later Dad knocked.
"Come on in, it's unlocked."
"Hello, princess, how are you?"
"We are all good, you need to speak to me about something?"
"Yes."
"Let's sit on the sofa so you can be comfortable," he said. "I'm
all ears."
"Shun had a discussion today, he was concerned about being
able to come over and visit with us and help out. You know
Mom said he nor his family is welcome here, so we just left it at
that, but the now the time is close and Mom hasn't come
around. He doesn't know what to expect and he doesn't want to
wait until I am driving again to be able to be with us. I have
been praying to be okay with the problems with her. I'm at the
end and she hasn't shown any love or concern for us, so I pray
all the time that this doesn't affect our relationship afterwards.
Dad, I know that I disappointed the both o you, you have forgiven me, and I have forgiven myself. You never made me feel
that you stopped loving me. I'm not perfect by a long shot, it
helps make me feel better about what I've done and to know
that you support me and have my back it give me strength to
make it and to keep moving forward. As I said I'm only staying
out of school the allotted time and then right back at it. I'm
going to graduate on time. I'm studying and keeping up with all
of my assignments. I'm making straight A's and I'm going on to
college, not out of town now because I'm not going to be away

from my babies, so what do you have to say?"

"As you know I apologize for your mother. I too am hurt by her actions. I thought she would have come around by now. I started off by not mentioning the pregnancy to her at first to give her time to process things, thinking sooner or later she would bring it up, but as time went by it never happened. She hasn't tried any more tricks, I don't think, but she is close-mouthed, she doesn't say much."

"I don't ever see you talking to her or checking on you now and I try not to keep my focus on that. I feel so bad about this. I know you are sad and you are sorry on her behalf, but you are not responsible for her. She's not even sorry for her own actions, at least she's not showing that she is. As far as I'm concerned it is what it is, I just need some answers as it relates to after we come home and anyway, Dad, you already know that everybody knows about me, they have seen me and people talk wherever you go, the neighbors at school, the hiding was over long ago, even then I wasn't hiding. I just wasn't showing and they are not perfect either, we need to ask Mom if she ever disappointed her parents or herself. I'm sure it's the same with you, you have to first of all ask for forgiveness, then forgive, then make the best of it."

"You are so right, Beth, I am going to speak to her, letting her know about what we've talked about, and I'm letting her know that the whole family will be welcome here. She shouldn't have a problem with Mi'lan because that was all her doings, so you can feel some relief. Shun can visit as much as he needs to."

"Thank you, because the thought had entered my mind to petition the courts to be on my own. I had looked into it even though I knew I could talk to you, I hadn't said anything to anybody about it and I didn't want you hurt by my actions. You have never left my side and you are trying to right every wrong, and I love you even more for it. You make me feel like we can make horrible mistakes and move past them, so trusting God and having you stick by me gives me strength to keep moving."

CHAPTER 52

Today was Saturday and it was time for my visit with Doctor Rancifer. I was about to go down for breakfast. I had about an hour and a half before I left. I was feeling okay so I decided to drive myself. Shun was lucky enough to work half a day so he could go with me. I was happy about that. He missed the last one. Symie had something to come up unexpected so she wasn't able to come with me. She asked if Jeffrey was driving me. I told her, "No, I'll be all right, just needed him to put my bags in the car, like you said you never know what will happen."

I sat down to eat, seemed like I couldn't get full. I ate so much, I thought I would burst. Just as I finished, Mom walked in. She looked at my stomach and I could see her gasp. Maybe she was just noticing how huge I was. I said hi and she said hello and stalled for a minute, but she said nothing else so I went out to my car. I had to scoop Shun up and head on out.

Symie was standing by the door. "Are you sure you should be doing this alone?"

I said, "I'm good, Shun will be in here with me real soon, we will get a bite to eat and walk in the park afterwards, I won't be out late. I'll be back before dark. You're a doll to be concerned about me but I'm fine and I will be fine. It's sad you show more love and compassion for me than my own mother. She was just now looking at me as if she's never seen a belly before, so I'll do what I've been doing all along, keep praying for her and asking God for continued peace for myself, so I'm off now. I have my cell phone and you can check on me whenever you like if it will make you feel better, and you know that I am going to."